CONTEMPORARY
SHORT STORIES

SELECTED AND EDITED BY
E. R. WOOD, B.A.
DEPUTY HEADMASTER
THE HIGH SCHOOL FOR BOYS
HEREFORD

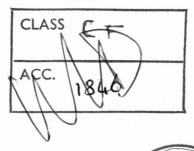
London . **BLACKIE & SON LIMITED** . Glasgow

First published, 1958
Reprinted, 1960

Printed in Great Britain by Blackie & Son, Ltd., Glasgow

CONTENTS

PREFACE

This book is intended to be enjoyed by boys and girls in the upper forms of grammar schools. Stories that are too subtle or too adult in their appeal have not been included, and it has been assumed that young readers will prefer a strong narrative interest, even if this quality is not entirely typical of contemporary writing. Within this limitation, a representative collection is offered of stories of the last twenty years, both by established authors whose names at once come to mind when the short story form is mentioned, and by others of a newly emerging generation. There is a varied assortment of types of narration and of prose styles, and a rich variety of experience to stir the imagination of the modern reader.

E. R. W.

ACKNOWLEDGMENTS

The Editor and Publishers desire to make grateful acknowledgment to the following for permission to reprint copyright material from the works named:

Mr. H. E. Bates and Messrs. Jonathan Cape, Ltd., for 'Sergeant Carmichael' from *How Sleep the Brave*.

Mr. T. O. Beachcroft and Messrs. John Lane The Bodley Head, Ltd., for 'The Half-Mile' from the author's *Collected Stories*.

Miss Phyllis Bottome and Messrs. Faber and Faber, Ltd., for 'Caesar's Wife's Ear' from *Man and Beast*.

Mr. John Brophy for 'The Prodigal Calf'.

Mr. J. A. B. Cuddon for 'Jumping for Joy'.

Mr. C. S. Forester for 'The Examination for Lieutenant' from *Mr. Midshipman Hornblower* published by Messrs. Michael Joseph, Ltd.

Miss Stella Gibbons and Messrs. Longmans, Green & Co., Ltd., for 'Saturday Afternoon' from *Roaring Tower and Other Stories*.

Mr. Desmond Hawkins for 'A Man and a Fox'.

Mr. E. L. Malpass and Messrs. William Heinemann, Ltd., for 'Return of the Moon Man' from *A.D. 2500*.

Miss Audrie Manley-Tucker for 'Wanted—A Miracle'.

Mr. Frank O'Connor for 'The Man of the House' from *Traveller's Samples*.

Mr. L. A. G. Strong and Messrs. Methuen & Co., Ltd., for 'The Gates' from *The Travellers*.

INTRODUCTION

The short story, like the novel, the theatre and the cinema, provides a means of living snatches of other people's lives. This substitute for real experience may be in strange or even sensational worlds far from our ordinary existence; after reading this book, for instance, you will know how it feels to face angry lions in a circus, to make your first parachute jump, or to drift in a rubber dinghy from a ditched aircraft. In a more humdrum sphere you may come home to Saturday tea after seeing your favourite soccer team win, or, inside the mind of Beachcroft's athlete, you may go through the nervous strain and excitement of running and winning the half-mile.

We are all gluttons for experience: when we are not busy living our own lives we are eager to live other people's—without, of course, the hardships and dangers and entanglements of the reality. The interest of such experience may be in the thrill of events, so that we avidly read on to know what happens next; or in the intensity or clarity with which the 'feel' of the experience is captured; or in subtle shades of emotion and atmosphere. We may explore with unusual understanding the mind of a child in 'The Man of the House' or that of an ageing man in 'The Gates'.

One of our standards for judging literature is the *quality* of the experience—whether it moves us and whether it is worth our absorption in it. If in our reading we are preoccupied with murderers evading

1

detectives or cowboys defying sheriffs, our substitute-experience is limited and distorted, and its values are often naïve or crude. For the writer, as well as giving us a little of someone else's life to live, is making directly or indirectly some comment on this life, leaving us to draw conclusions about how life ought to be lived and what makes human beings act as they do. The quality of this comment—whether it is wise or wrongheaded, original or commonplace, inspiring or cynical—forms another possible standard of judgment.

So much for the matter of literature. The manner of telling is important too; the pleasure that we gain from reading clearly depends on the skill and method of the story-teller. Some stories, for example, are told *from the inside*, so that as we read we become in imagination the person to whom things are happening (often the 'I' of the story): in others the writer stands *outside* his characters (and the reader with him), remaining objective or approving, criticizing, even ridiculing. In the former type the reader probably lives the story more intensely: in the latter the writer has more resources at his command; he can intervene as himself, stop the story while he has a word with the reader, then turn to another thread of his tale; as he is omniscient, he can move back in time or give us hints of what is to come later, and he can get inside the minds of his characters one by one and tell us what they are thinking; his own personality—or a personality which he assumes for the purposes of the story—may also enrich our impressions. To the appreciation of these various methods of unfolding events and giving interesting pattern and meaning to them, we must add the pleasure to be had from sheer style, the author's way of managing words, sentences and images.

What has been said so far applies to literature generally. When we seek standards by which to consider short stories, we need to ask ourselves what makes the short story a separate form, and this is not an easy question to answer. A short story, most readers would agree, is not an abbreviated novel. A novel of three hundred pages or more is evidently built on different lines from anything in this book; in a work of such scope the characters can be more profoundly explored and the interplay of personalities usually creates a little community—the Barchester of Trollope's novels, the London of Galsworthy's Forsyte family, or the elegant, narrow world of Jane Austen; the scheme of events may extend elaborately over time and space to include many generations or several lands; a serious novelist's comment on life may assume the importance of a philosophy. The short story is not a mere skeleton of all this, any more than a sonnet is a skeleton ode. The small compass dictates both the matter found suitable and the manner of the telling. An obvious virtue will be in the selection of incident that can be complete in confined space, the choice of characters capable of being presented as real and rounded but without complications or subtleties, and then the packing into a small space of just the right amount of development in the right proportions of this material.

When nineteenth-century novelists wrote short

stories most of them, from Scott at the beginning of
the century to Stevenson at the end, followed much
the same lines as in novels; they began with one or
two pages of description of persons or places,
elaborated detail at leisure, even divided the story
into chapters. Short story writers of today move more
nimbly, explaining and describing less, expecting the
reader to grasp at hints and deft strokes. In this the
short story resembles the film; the cinema audience
is accustomed to seizing upon the implications of
details without needing to have them explained. You
will see how rapidly the stories in this book get into
motion, with what economy such characters as Mrs.
Spenk, Seppel or Sergeant Carmichael are brought to
life. Like the film, the successful short story has
usually one central theme or character kept sharply
in focus; it is like the film, too, in its completeness,
in our feeling at the end that the incident is over.

These positive qualities of the short story are not
rigidly established and the form is all the more
indefinite because of changing fashions and standards
of judgment. In the past, writers made incident the
essence of story-telling, and in shaping a pattern of
events story-tellers like O. Henry developed a popular
form in which everything led up to an unexpected
twist or revelation at the end. But there has been in
the last quarter-century a reaction against this kind of
plot-manipulation, which could, it must be admitted,
become too mechanical or strained. A neat plot,
once thought essential, came to be looked on with
disdain. Extreme developments of this reaction pro-
duced blurred fragments without apparent shape or

coherence, pieces in which little or nothing happens but a slanting light is cast mistily on aspects of human life. For the purposes of this collection, however, it has been assumed that a clear chain of incident should form the core of a short story. But this is no longer enough. Contemporary writers, weary of the hackneyed plots and contrived crises which older story-tellers had fully exploited, have extended the frontiers of the short story form, as can be seen here. They have sought above all sincerity, sensitiveness, freshness; they have striven to achieve the intangible quality called atmosphere; and they have explored strange motives and moods of human beings to enlarge our understanding of our kind.

H. E. BATES

SERGEANT CARMICHAEL

H. E. Bates was born in 1905 at Northampton, and went to Kettering Grammar School. He began work as a provincial journalist and later became a warehouse clerk, but his gifts as a writer were soon recognized and he was only twenty years old when his first novel, The Two Sisters, *was published. He became a very successful writer of short stories, especially about country people.*

H. E. Bates has written: 'I have never from the first had the slightest interest in plots . . . The idea of plots is something completely foreign to my whole conception of the short story.' He was primarily interested in mood, character and atmosphere. In his early stories he showed (he says) 'a dangerous appetite for sucking the significance out of trivialities,' and although, according to him, it was this eager interest in trivialities that made him a short story writer, it threatened to limit his scope.

'Sergeant Carmichael' shows us a new Bates, for the War of 1939-45 extended his scope, opening fresh worlds of inspiration. In 1941 he joined the Royal Air Force and under the pseudonym of 'Flying Officer X' he wrote two immensely popular books of stories about fighter pilots and bomber crews, The Greatest People in the World *(1942) and* How Sleep the Brave *(1943). Later, under his own name, he published three exciting yet sensitive war novels,* Fair Stood the Wind for France, The Purple

Plain *and* The Jacaranda Tree, *which won him a new and very wide reputation.*

Collections of his short stories include Thirty Tales, My Uncle Silas, *and* Country Tales. *He has also written a book on the modern short story.*

●

For some time he had had a feeling that none of them knew where they were going. They had flown over France without seeing land. Now they were flying in heavy rain without a glimpse of the sea. He was very young, just twenty, and suddenly he had an uneasy idea that they would never see either the land or the sea again.

'Transmitter pretty u.s.,[1] sir,' he said.

For a moment there was no answer. Then Davidson, the captain, answered automatically, 'Keep trying, Johnnie,' and he answered 'O.K.', quite well knowing there was nothing more to do. He sat staring straight before him. Momentarily he was no longer part of the aircraft. He was borne away from it on sound-waves of motors and wind and rain, and for a few minutes he was back in England, recalling and re-living odd moments of life there. He recalled for a second or two his first day on the station; it was August and he remembered that some straw had blown in from the fields across the runways and that the wind of the take-offs whirled it madly upward, yellow and shining in the sun. He recalled his father eating red currants in the garden that same summer and how the crimson juice had spurted on to his moustache, so that he looked rather ferocious every time he said, 'That, if you want it, is my opinion.' And then he remembered, most curiously of all, a girl in a biscuit-yellow hat sitting in a deckchair on the sea-front, eating a biscuit-yellow ice-cream, and how he had been fascinated because hat and ice were miraculously identical in colour and how he had wanted to ask her, with nervous bravado because he was very young, if she bought her hats to match her ice-cream or her ice-cream to match her hats, but how he never did. He did not know why he recalled these moments, clear as glass, except perhaps that they were moments of a life he was never going to see again.

He was suddenly ejected out of this past world, fully alert and aware that they were not flying straight. They had not been flying straight for some time. They were stooging round[2] and round, bumping heavily, and losing height. He sat very tense, and became gradually aware that this tension was part of the plane. It existed in each of them from Davidson and Porter in the nose, down through Johnson and Hargreaves and himself to Carmichael in the tail.

He heard Davidson's voice. 'How long since we had contact with base?'

He looked at his watch; it was almost midnight. 'A little under an hour and three-quarters,' he said.

Again there was silence; and again he felt the tension running through the 'plane. He was aware of their chances and almost aware, now, of what Davidson was going to say.

'One more try, boys. Sing out if you see anything. If not it's down in the drink.'[3]

He sat very still. They were losing a little height. His stomach felt sour and he remembered that he could not swim.

For some reason he never thought of it again. His thoughts were scattered by Davidson's voice.

'Does anyone see what I see? Isn't that a light? About two points to starboard.'

He looked out; there was nothing he could see.

'I'm going down to have a look-see,' Davidson said. 'It *is* a light.'

As they were going down he looked out again, but again he could see nothing. Then he heard Davidson speaking to Carmichael.

'Hack the fuselage door off, Joe. This looks like a light-ship. If it is we're as good as home. Tell me when you're ready and I'll put her down.'

He sat very still, hearing the sound of hatchet blows as Carmichael struck at the fuselage. He felt suddenly colder, and then knew that it must be because Carmichael had finished and that there was a gap where the door had been. He heard again the deep slow Canadian accent of Carmichael's voice, saying, 'O.K., skipper, all set,' and then the remote flat English voice of Davidson in reply:

'All right, get the dinghy[4] ready. All three of you. Get ready and heave it out when I put her down.'

Helping Joe and Hargreaves and Johnson with the dinghy he was no longer aware of fear. He was slung sideways across the aircraft. There was not much room. The dinghy seemed very large and he wondered how they would get it out. This troubled him until he felt the 'plane roaring down in the darkness, and it continued to trouble him for a second after the 'plane had hit the water with a crash that knocked him back against the fuselage. He did not remember getting up. Something was wrong with his left wrist, and he thought of his watch. It was a good watch, given him by his father on a birthday. The next moment he knew that the dinghy had gone and he knew that he had helped, somehow, to push it out. Carmichael had also gone. The sea was rocking the aircraft violently to and fro, breaking water against his knees and feet. A second later he stretched out his hands and felt nothing before him but the open space in the fuselage where the door had been.

He knew then that it must be his turn to go. He heard Carmichael's voice calling from what seemed a great distance out of the darkness and the rain. He did not know what he was calling. It was all confused; he did not answer, but a second later he stretched out his hands blindly and went down on his belly on the sea.

II

When he came up again it was to find himself thinking of the girl in the biscuit-coloured hat and how much, that day, he had liked the sea, opaque and green and smooth as the pieces of sea-washed glass he had picked up on the shore. It flashed through his mind that this was part of the final

imagery that comes with drowning, and he struggled
wildly to keep his face above water. He could hear
again the voice of Carmichael, shouting, but the
shock of sea-water struck like ice on his breast and
throat, so that he could not shout in answer. The sea
was very rough. It heaved him upwards and then down
again with sweeps of slow and violent motion. It
tossed him about in this way until he realized at last
that these slow, barbaric waves were really keeping
him up, that the Mae West[5] was working and that he
was sinking away no longer.

From the constancy of Carmichael's shouts he felt
that Carmichael must have seized, and was probably on, the dinghy. But he was not prepared for the
shout: 'She's upside down!' and then a moment
or two later two voices yelling his name.

'Johnny! Can you hear us? Can you hear us now?'

He let out a great yell in answer but the sea-water
broke down his throat, for a moment suffocated him,
bearing him down and under the trough of a wave.
He came up sick and struggling, spitting water,
frightened. His boots were very heavy now under the
water and it seemed as if he were being sucked continually down. He tried to wave his arms above his
head but one arm had no response. It filled him
suddenly with violent pain.

'O.K., Johnny, O.K., O.K.,' Carmichael said.

He could not speak. He knew that his arm was
broken. He felt Carmichael's hands painfully clutching
his one free hand. He remembered for no reason at
all that Carmichael had been pitcher for a baseball
team in Montreal, and he felt the hands move down

until they clutched his wrist, holding him so strongly that it was almost a pain.

'Can you bear up?' Carmichael said. 'Johnny, try bearing up. It's O.K. We're here, on the dinghy. Hargreaves is here. Johnson's here. We're all here except the skipper. It's O.K., Johnny. Can you heave? Where's your other arm?'

'I think it's burst,' he said.

He tried heaving himself upward. He tried again, helped by Carmichael's hands, but something each time drew the dinghy away. He tried again and then again. Each time the same thing happened, and once or twice the sea, breaking on the dinghy, hit him in the face, blinding him.

He knew suddenly what was wrong. It was not only his arm but his belt. Each time he heaved upwards the belt caught under the dinghy and pushed it away. In spite of knowing it he heaved again and all at once felt very tired, feeling that only Carmichael's hands were between his tiredness and instant surrender. This painful heaving and sudden tiredness were repeated. They went on for some time. He heard Carmichael's voice continually and once or twice the sea hit him again, blinding him, and once, blinded badly, he wanted to wipe his face with his hands.

Suddenly Carmichael was talking again. 'Can you hang on? If I can get my knee on something I'll get leverage. I'll pull you up. Can you hang on?'

Before he could answer the sea hit him again. The waves seemed to split his contact with Carmichael. It momentarily cut away his hands. For an instant it was as if he were in a bad and terrifying dream, falling through space.

Then Carmichael was holding him again. 'I got you now, Johnny. I'm kneeling on Dicky. Your belt ought to clear now. If you try hard it ought to clear first time.'

The sea swung him away. As he came back the belt did not hit the dinghy so violently. He was kept almost clear. Then the sea swung him away again. On this sudden wave of buoyancy he realized that it was now, or perhaps never, that he must pull himself back. He clenched his hand violently; and then suddenly before he was ready, and very lightly as if he were a child, the force of the new wave and the strength of Carmichael's hands threw him on the dinghy, face down.

He wanted to lie there for a long time. He lay for only a second, and then got up. He felt the water heaving in his boots and the salt sickness of it in his stomach. He did not feel at all calm but was terrified for an instant by the shock of being safe.

'There was a light,' he said. 'That's why he came down here. That's why he came down. There was a light.'

He looked around at the sea as he spoke. Sea and darkness were one, unbroken except where waves struck the edge of the dinghy with spits of faintly phosphorescent foam. It had ceased raining now but the wind was very strong and cold, and up above lay the old unbroken ten-tenths cloud. There was not even a star that could have been mistaken for a light. He knew that perhaps there never had been.

He went into a slight stupor brought on by pain and the icy sea-water. He came out of it to find himself furiously baling water from the dinghy with one hand. He noticed that the rest were baling with their caps. He had lost his cap. His one hand made a nerveless cup that might have been stone for all the feeling that was in it now.

The sea had a rhythmical and awful surge that threw the dinghy too lightly up the glassy arcs of oncoming waves and then too steeply over the crest into the trough beyond. Each time they came down into a trough the dinghy shipped a lot of water. Each time they baled frenziedly, sometimes throwing the water over each other. His good hand remained dead. He still did not feel the water with it but he felt it on his face, sharp as if the spray were splintered and frozen glass. Then whenever they came to the crest of a wave there was a split second when they could look for a light. 'Hell, there should be a light,' he thought. 'He saw one. He shouted it out. That's why he came down,' but each time the sea beyond the crest of the new wave remained utterly dark as before.

'What the hell,' he said. 'There should be a light! There *was* a light.'

'All right, kid,' Carmichael said. 'There'll be one.'

He knew then that he was excited. He tried not to be excited. For a long time he didn't speak, but his mind remained excited. He felt drunk with the motion of pain and the water and sick with the saltness of the water. There were moments when he ceased baling and held his one hand strengthlessly at his side, tired out, wanting to give up. He did not know how he kept going after a time or how they kept the water from swamping the dinghy.

Coming out of periods of stupor, he would hear Carmichael talking. The deep Canadian voice was slow and steady. It attracted him. He found himself listening simply to the sound and the steadiness of it, regardless of words. It had the quality of Carmichael's hands; it was calm and steadfast.

It occurred to him soon that the voice had another quality. It was like the baling of the water; it never stopped. He heard Carmichael talking of ball games in Montreal; the way the crowd ragged you and how you took no notice and how it was all part of the game; and then how he was injured in the game one summer and for two months couldn't play and how he went up into Quebec province for the fishing. It was hot weather and he would fish mostly in the late evenings, often by moonlight. The lake trout were big and strong and sometimes a fish took you an hour to get in. Sometimes at weekends he went back to Quebec and he would eat steaks as thick, he said, as a volume of Dickens and rich with onions and butter. They were lovely with cold light beer, and the whole thing set you back about two dollars and a half.

'Good eh, Johnny?' he would say. 'You ought to come over there some day.'

All the time they baled furiously. There was no break in the clouds and the wind was so strong that it sometimes swivelled the dinghy round like a toy.

How long this went on he did not know. But a long time later Carmichael suddenly stopped talking and then as suddenly began again.

'Hey, Johnny boy, there's your light!'

He was startled and looked up wildly, not seeing anything.

'Not that way, boy. Back of you. Over there.'

He turned his head stiffly. There behind him he could see the dim cream edge of daylight above the line of the sea.

'That's the light we want,' Carmichael said. 'It don't go out in a hurry either.'

The colour of daylight was deeper, like pale butter, when he looked over his shoulder again. He remembered then that it was late summer. He thought that now, perhaps, it would be three o'clock.

As the daylight grew stronger, changing from cream and yellow to a cool grey bronze, he saw for the first time the barbaric quality of the sea. He saw the faces of Carmichael and Hargreaves and Johnson. They were grey-yellow with weariness and touched at the lips and ears and under the eyes with blue.

He was very thirsty. He could feel a thin caking of salt on his lips. He tried to lick his lips with his tongue, but it was very painful. There was no moisture on his tongue and only the taste of salt, very harsh and bitter, in his mouth. His arm was swollen and he was sick with pain.

'Take it easy a minute, kid,' Carmichael said. 'We'll bale in turns. You watch out for a ship or a kite[6] or anything you can see. I'll tell you when it's your turn.'

He sat on the edge of the dinghy and stared at the horizon and the sky. Both were empty. He rubbed the salt out of his eyes and then closed them for a moment, worn out.

'Watch out,' Carmichael said. 'We're in the Channel. We know that. There should be ships and there should be aircraft. Keep watching.'

He kept watching. His eyes were painful with salt and only half-open. Now and then the sea hit the dinghy and broke right over it, but he did not care. For some reason he did not think of listening, but suddenly he shut his eyes and after a moment or two he heard a sound. It was rather like the sound of the sea beating gently on sand, and he remembered again the day when he had seen the girl in the biscuit-coloured hat and how it was summer and how much he had liked the sea. That day the sea had beaten on the shore with the same low sound.

As the sound increased he suddenly opened his eyes. He felt for a moment that he was crazy and then he began shouting.

'It's a 'plane! It's a bloody 'plane! It's a 'plane, I tell you, it's a 'plane!'

'Sit down,' Carmichael said.

The dinghy was rocking violently. The faces of all four were upturned, grey-yellow in the stronger light.

'There she is!' he shouted. 'There she is!'

The 'plane was coming over from the north-east, at about five thousand. He began to wave his hands. She seemed to be coming straight above them. Hargreaves and Johnson and then Carmichael also began to wave. They all waved frantically and Hargreaves shouted, 'It's a Hudson, boys. Wave like raving Hallelujah! It's a Hudson.'

The 'plane came over quite fast and very steady, flying straight. It looked the colour of iron except for the bright rings of the markings in the dull sea-light of the early morning. It flew on quite straight and they were still waving frantically with their hands and caps long after it had ceased looking like a far-off gull in the sky.

He came out of the shock of this disappointment to find that Carmichael was holding him in the dinghy with one arm.

'I'm all right,' he said.

'I know,' Carmichael said.

He knew then that he was not all right. He felt dizzy. A slow river of cold sweat seemed to be pouring from his hair down his backbone.

'What happened?' he said.

'You're all right,' Carmichael said. 'Don't try to stand up again, that's all. How's your arm? I wish there was something I could do.'

'It's O.K.,' he said.

He remembered the 'plane. The sky was now quite light, barred with warm strips of orange low above the water in the east. He remembered also that it was summer. The wind was still strong and cold but soon, he thought, there will be sun. He looked overhead and knew now that it would be a fair day for flying.

'Does the sun rise in the east or a little to the north-east?' Carmichael said.

They held a little discussion, and Johnny and Hargreaves agreed that in summer it rose a little to the north-east.

'In that case we seem to be drifting almost due north. If the wind helps us we might drift into the coast. It's still strong.'

'It's about forty,' Hargreaves said. 'It must have been about eighty last night.'

'It was a point or two west of south then,' Johnny said.

'I think it's still there,' Carmichael said.

They all spoke rather slowly. His own lips felt huge and dry with blisters. It was painful for him to speak. He was not hungry, but the back of his throat was scorched and raw with salt. His tongue was thick and hot and he wanted to roll it out of his mouth, so that it would get sweet and cool in the wind.

'Keep your mouth shut, Johnny,' Carmichael said. 'Keep it shut.'

He discovered that Carmichael was still holding him by the arm. In the hour or two that went by between the disappearance of the Hudson and the time when the sun was well up and he could feel the warmth of it on his face he continually wanted to protest; to tell Carmichael that he was all right. Yet he never did and all the time Carmichael held him and he was glad.

All the time they watched the sea and the sky and most of the time Carmichael talked to them. He talked to them again of Canada, the lakes in the summertime, the fishing, the places where you could eat in Montreal. The sea was less violent now, but the waves, long and low and metallically glittering in the sun, swung the dinghy ceaselessly up and down troughs that bristled with destructive edges of foam. Towards the middle of the morning Hargreaves was very sick. He leaned his head forward on his knees and sat very quiet for a long time, too weak to lift his head. The sickness itself became covered and churned and finally washed away by incoming water. After this only Johnson and Carmichael troubled to watch the horizon, and they took turns at baling the water, Carmichael using one hand.

For some time none of them spoke. Finally when Johnny looked up again it was to see that Johnson too had closed his eyes against the glitter of sunlight and only Carmichael was watching the sea. He was watching in a curious attitude. As he held Johnny with one hand he would lean forward and with his hat bale a little water out of the dinghy. Then he would transfer the hat from one hand to the other and with the free hand press the fabric of the dinghy as you press the inner tube of a tyre. As he pressed it seemed flabby. Then he would look up and gaze for a few moments at the horizon, northwards, where at intervals the sea seemed to crystallize into long lips of misty grey. For a long time Johnny sat watching him, following the movements of his hands and the arrested progress of his eyes.

Very slowly he realized what was happening. He did not move. He wanted to speak but the back of his throat was raw and his tongue was thick and inflexible. When he suddenly opened his mouth his lips split and there was blood in the cracks that was bitterly salt as he licked it with his tongue.

He did not know which struck him first: the realization that the thin lips of grey on the horizon were land or that the dinghy was losing air. For a second or two his emotions were cancelled out. The dinghy was upside down; the bellows were gone.

He felt slightly light-headed. Above the horizon the
clouds were white-edged now, and suddenly the sun
broke down through them and shone on the line of
land turning the lips of grey to brown. He knew
then that it was land. There could be no mistake. But
looking down suddenly into the dinghy he knew that
there was and could be no mistake there either.

He began to shout. He did not know what he
shouted. His mouth was very painful. He rocked his
body forward and began to bale excitedly with his free
hand. In a moment the rest were shouting too.

'Steady,' Carmichael said, 'steady.'

'How far is it away?' Hargreaves said. 'Five miles?
Five or six?'

'Nearer ten.'

'I'll take a bet.'

'You'd better take one on the air in the dinghy.'

It was clear that Hargreaves did not know about the
air in the dinghy. He ceased baling and sat very tense.
His tongue was thick and grey-pink and hanging out
of his mouth.

It seemed to Johnny that the dinghy, slowly losing
resilience, was like something dying underneath
them.

'Now don't anybody go and get excited,' Carmichael said. 'We must be drifting in fast, and if we
drift in far enough and she gives out we can swim.
You all better bale now while you can. All right,
Johnny? Can you bale?'

Baling frantically with his one hand, looking up at
intervals at the horizon, now like a thin strip of
cream-brown paint squeezed along the edge of the sea,

he tried not to think of the fact that he could not swim.

All the time he felt the dinghy losing air. He felt its flabbiness grow in proportion to his own weight. It moved very heavily and sluggishly in the troughs of water, and waves broke over it more often now. Sometimes the water rose almost to the knees of the men. He could not feel his feet and several times it seemed as if the bottom of the dinghy had fallen out and that beneath him there was nothing but the bottom of the sea.

It went on like this for a long time, the dinghy losing air, the land coming a little nearer, deeper-coloured now, with veins of grey.

'God, we'll never make it,' Hargreaves said. 'We'll never make it.'

Carmichael did not speak. The edge of the dinghy was low against the water, almost level. The sea lapped over it constantly and it was more now than they could bale.

Johnny looked at the land. The sun was shining down on smooth uplands of green and calm brown squares of upturned earth. Below lay long chalk cliffs, changing from sea-grey to white in the sun. He felt suddenly exhausted and desperate. He felt that he hated the sea. He was frightened of it and suddenly lost his head and began to bale with one arm, throwing the water madly everywhere.

'We'll never do it!' he shouted. 'We'll never do it. Why the hell didn't that Hudson see us? What the hell do they do in those fancy kites?'

'Shut up,' Carmichael said.

He felt suddenly quiet and frightened.

3

'Shut up. She's too heavy, that's all. Take your boots off.'

Hargreaves and Johnson stopped baling and took off their boots. He tried to take off his own boots but they seemed part of his feet and with only one arm he was too weak to pull them off. Then Carmichael took off his own boots. He took off his socks too, and Johnny could see that Carmichael's feet were blue and dead.

For a minute he could not quite believe what he saw next. He saw Carmichael roll over the side of the dinghy into the sea. He went under and came up again at once, shaking the water from his hair. 'O.K.,' he shouted, 'O.K. Keep baling. I'm pushing her in. She'll be lighter now.

Carmichael put his hands on the end of the dinghy and swam with his feet.

'I'm coming over too,' Hargreaves said.

'No. Keep baling. Keep her light. There'll be time to come over.'

They went on like this for some time. The situation in the dinghy was bad, but he did not think of it. His knees were sometimes wholly submerged and the dinghy was flabby and without life. All the time he hated the sea and kept his eyes in desperation on the shore. Then Carmichael gave Hargreaves the order to go over and Hargreaves rolled over the side as Carmichael had done and came up soon and began swimming in the same way.

They were then about five hundred yards from the shore and they could see sheep in the fields above the cliffs, but no houses. The land looked washed and bright and for some reason abandoned, as if no one had ever set foot there. The sea was calm now, but it still washed over the dinghy too fast for him to bale and he still hated it. Then suddenly Johnson went over the side without waiting for a word from Carmichael, and he was alone in the dinghy, being pushed along by the three men. But he knew that it could not last. The dinghy was almost flat, and between the force of the three men pushing and the resistance of the water it crumpled and submerged and would not move.

As if there were something funny about this Johnson began laughing. He himself felt foolish and scared and waited with clenched teeth for the dinghy to go down.

It went down before he was ready, throwing him backwards. He felt a wave hit him and then he went under, his boots dragging him down. He struggled violently and quite suddenly saw the sky. His arm was very painful and he felt lop-sided. He was lying on his back and he knew that he was moving, not of his own volition but easily and strongly, looking at the lakes of summer sky between the white and indigo hills of cloud. He was uneasy and glad at the same time. The sea still swamped over his face, scorching his broken lips, but he was glad because he knew that Carmichael was holding him again and taking him in to shore.

What seemed a long time later he knew that they were very near the shore. He heard the loud warm sound of breaking waves. He was borne forward in long surges of the tide. At last he could no longer feel Carmichael's arms, but tired, and kept up by his Mae West[5], he drifted in of his own accord. The sun was strong on his face and he thought suddenly of the things he had thought about in the 'plane: the straw on the runways, his father eating the currants, the girl in the biscuit-coloured hat. He felt suddenly that they were the things for which he had struggled. They were his life. The waves took him gradually farther and farther up the shore, until his knees beat on the sand. He saw Carmichael and Johnson and Hargreaves waiting on the shore. At last new waves took him far up the shore until he lay still on the wet slope of sand and his arms were outstretched to the sky.

As he lay there the sea ran down over his body and receded away. It was warm and gentle on his hands and he was afraid of it no longer.

Notes

1. *u.s.*: unserviceable, out of order.
2. *Stooging round*: flying aimlessly, not on a proper course.
3. *In the drink*: in the sea.
4. *Dinghy*: an inflated rubber raft, carried in aircraft for emergencies.
5. *Mae West*: an inflated life-belt, like a waistcoat, so-called after a buxom film actress.
6. *Kite*: an aircraft.

T. O. BEACHCROFT

THE HALF-MILE

T. O. Beachcroft was born in 1902 and was educated at Clifton and at Balliol College, Oxford. At Oxford he ran the mile and the half-mile for the University. He has worked for the B.B.C. as a news reader and announcer and is now Chief Overseas Publicity Officer. He was a regular contributor of literary criticism to The Criterion *under the editorship of T. S. Eliot and he was the editor of the first fifty numbers of the British Council series of short studies entitled* Writers and Their Work. *For the past thirty years his short stories have been appearing in publications in Britain and America and he has published several volumes, including* A Young Man in a Hurry *(1934) and* Collected Stories *(1946). This story is a good example of his gift for 'living' his characters so that the reader does so too.*

●

Saturday noon. The town hall clock boomed the hour in the distance. All over the town, hooters called to each other from street to street. From the gates of twenty different potteries, men, women, boys, and girls streamed. Ones and twos grew to a steady flow, then died away again to ones and twos.

Andrew Williamson, a dipper at the Royal Chorley,

was stopped at the gate by old Jones the doorkeeper.

'So long, Andrew,' he said, 'good luck for the half-mile.'

Andrew glanced at him, and looked away self-consciously.

'How did you know I was running?'

'Oh, I takes an interest,' said Joe, 'used to run a half-mile myself.'

'Go on?' said Andrew. 'I never knew.'

'I was good for one-fifty-eight,' said the old man. 'That was good going in those days.'

'Go on?' said Andrew again, 'but that's class running. That's a class half-mile.'

'Oh, I dunno, plenty on 'em do it now!'

'Well, I wish I could. That's my ambition: to get inside two minutes. I've never beaten two-four yet!'

'Well, this is just the day for it,' the veteran told him. 'You have a nice trot round first: get some good summer air into your lungs: you'll win.'

'But I've never run in a class race,' Andrew persisted. 'I've only done Club races. I can't hope for more'n a place; look who's running.'

'Who?' said Jones.

'Well, there's six of us in the final. Let's see: Joe Brewster, the cross-country man; he can run a four-thirty mile, and now he wants to try the half.'

'Well, he'll never do two minutes,' said Jones, 'take it from me.'

'Then there's Perry, him as ran at the "Three Clubs" meet at Derby last week. He did two-four then.'

'Well, who else?'

'There's that Redbrooke, the Cambridge Blue. I ain't got an earthly.'

'He's a fine runner,' said Jones, 'but d'you think he's trained in May? Not likely; it'll be his first time out—trial spin like. Are you trained?'

'Pretty good,' said Andrew, 'been at it evenings all the month. Had a good race a week ago.'

'Take it from me,' Jones told him slowly, 'stick to Redbrooke. He'll come up at the end of the first quarter. You watch 'im. Don't mind what the others do. And don't run on the outside round bends.'

'Well I know enough for that,' said Andrew.

'Ah, you know, you know,' said Jones. 'Well, good luck, lad.'

Andrew turned back again as he was going. 'If I could ever beat two minutes,' he said, a little self-consciously, 'it'd mean—oh, well, a lot.'

Andrew left him and went alone into the square garden to eat his sandwiches. It was a bright early summer day, yet now he was alone he felt chilly with nerves. He had a forty-minutes bus ride to the ground, and he meant to get there early. The half-mile was timed for three.

What chance had he got? He had won his heat in two-six the evening before, but that meant nothing. Joe Brewster was behind him, but he'd only paced it out, he knew. Perry and Redbrooke had tied the other heat in two-five. There was nothing to go by. Dreadful if he found himself outclassed and run off his legs. He had never been up against a class man before—a fellow like Redbrooke.

Once in the bus he tried his best not to think of the

race. No good getting too much of a needle. Yet it was a big chance.

Why, if he did well, if he was placed in the race to-day, his name would be in the *Sentinel*. The old 'uns would like to see that, too. If he could beat two minutes—well, he would some day, before he died. That would be doing something really big. It would give him confidence. It would make him stronger altogether.

The bus jogged along with such pleasant fancies. Andrew reached the ground, bag in hand, at half-past one. It gave him a queer feeling to see 'Sixpence Entrance' on the gates, and 'This stand a shilling', and the like. It made him feel very responsible that people should pay to come to the sport he was providing.

He was practically the first-comer in the changing-room. He changed slowly, putting his clothes on a bench in the corner. He put on his spiked shoes with elaborate care and went out on to the track. It was three laps to the mile instead of the four he was used to. Pity: every strangeness was a little disturbing in a race. There were not four corners either, but two long straights with a long semi-circular sweep at each end.

Andrew found the half-mile start, and took his bearings. He trotted round half a lap, took one or two sprints, then some breathing exercises. He paced up the back-straight. That was where he must come up to the front. He determined to make a real sprinting start, and get an inside berth at all costs. No need for old Jones to tell him not to run on the outside round bends. It was past two by now. One or two people were coming into the stands, the first event being at 2.30. When he got back to the changing-room he found it full of a noisy jostling crowd. He felt rather strange and out of it. If only he could get it over. Three-quarters of an hour to wait still. On a table a naked body was being massaged. Andrew waited his turn for a rub. This seemed really professional.

'Your turn, sir,' said the rubber.

Andrew stripped off his vest.

'Might as well take your bags off, too.'

He divested himself a bit shyly, and lay face downwards on the table.

'Front side first, old man,' said the rubber.

It seemed a bit indecent, but Andrew turned over.

The man pummelled his stomach, then his back, then his buttocks, his thighs and his calves, rubbing in a strong smelling oil that gingered up his skin and made his nerves tingle. Good.

He saw Brewster and Perry talking and made a remark to them about the half-mile, but they did not seem to remember who he was. He found himself a seat alone. If only he could get it over.

A red-faced man thrust the door open.

'All out for the hundred,' he shouted.

'Know who that is?' someone said. 'That's Major Cunliffe—the old international.'

The hundred-yards men trooped out. There were four or five heats in the hundred. Andrew watched out of the changing-room window, but he couldn't concentrate and took no stock of what happened. He was acutely miserable.

At last the hundred yards was finished. A minute or so dragged by. Andrew stood up and sat down again and fastened his shoes for the fifth time. Then the door burst open and Major Cunliffe looked in again.

'All out for the half-mile!'

At the same time he heard a bell ringing outside. It sounded fateful. *It meant next event due.* All over the ground people were turning over their programmes and reading the names. As the clangour died away Andrew felt something approaching terror. He sprang to his feet and crossed towards the door.

Now a new awkwardness arose. Why did none of the other half-milers move? He waited for a moment for them to join him, but each man of them seemed to have found some last-minute adjustment to a shoe or bandage.

'Well,' said Brewster, 'I suppose we'd better be moving.'

'Wait a bit, Joe,' said Perry, 'I must get my ankle strap on.'

Andrew hovered miserably in the doorway of the changing-room. Why couldn't they buck up and get it over? If only he could get it over. At last, finding it ridiculous to hold the door open any longer, he went through it and waited outside in the concrete passage. He certainly could not walk on to the track without the others, nor could he go back into the changing-room. He leant against the wall trying to think of nothing.

What could the others be doing? 'Oh, come on,'

he murmured, 'come on!' Next time he would know better than to get up before the other men in his race were on the move.

The sunlight end of the passage was suddenly eclipsed and the Major brushed by him.

'Where are those half-milers?' he said genially to Andrew.

'I think——' began Andrew, but found an answer was not expected.

The Major opened the door, and Andrew caught a glimpse of the bunch of them standing and talking as if the race meant nothing.

'Everyone out for the half-mile—come on, *please*,' said the Major.

This time they came, and with beating heart Andrew joined them.

'Well, Brewster,' said the Major, 'what are you going to show us today?'

'Don't expect you'll notice me,' said Brewster, 'after the gun's gone. I shall try and stick to young Redbrooke for the first six hundred, anyhow. I only want to see what I can do!'

It sounded splendidly casual, but Andrew had a strong feeling that what Brewster meant was: 'I rather fancy myself as a class half-miler, so just watch me. I believe I can beat Redbrooke. I'm not troubling about the rest, anyhow.'

Andrew stepped gingerly along the track. He felt rather better at being in the open air. Then he glanced behind him at the grandstand. He received a shock. It was full—full of banks of people looking at him, waiting to see him run.

With eyes fixed on the ground, he left the track and began to walk across the grass towards the start. The half-mile, being a lap and a half, led off at the farthest point from the grandstand. The half-lap brought it round to the stand just at the stage where the race was getting into its stride, when everybody was beginning to feel the collar and those who meant business were jostling for places in front. The remaining complete lap brought the finish round to the grandstand again.

Andrew's path took him into the middle of the ground; here the crowd was less imminent. The summer was still new enough to greet the senses with surprise. He stepped lightly on the elastic turf. The grass breathed out delicious freshness. For years afterwards that fragrance was to set Andrew's nerves tingling with the apprehension of this moment.

The lively air fanned his head and throat. It played about his bare legs.

Andrew saw the other half-milers were trotting round the track. Occasionally one would shoot forward in a muscle-stretching burst. Andrew tried a high-stepping trot across the grass to flex his own legs, but was too self-conscious to keep it up.

He reached the starting-point first. Another agonizing wait followed. The others were still capering round the path. Would he never get it over? Surely the tension of nerves must rack the strength from his limbs? At last the starter approached.

'Jolly day for a trial spin,' he told Andrew. 'Makes me feel an old fool to be out of it. I envy you boys.'

Andrew felt too miserable to answer. He nodded.

'If you want a place,' said the starter, 'take my advice and watch Redbrooke. He'll probably try to take Brewster off his legs early—he knows he can't sprint, you see.'

Andrew nodded again. Of course it was a foregone conclusion that only Redbrooke and Brewster were in the race. No one had a thought for him.

The others began to arrive. Andrew stripped off his sweater. Again he was premature. The others waited. All were silent now.

Redbrooke was strolling across the ground with one of the officials. He looked up and broke into a brisk trot.

The air still freshened Andrew's face. Across the ground he could hear the murmur of the crowd. A paper-boy was shouting.

Still none of the runners spoke. In silence, one by one, they took off blazers and sweaters. The well-known colours of Brewster's club appeared—a red and black band round the chest. Redbrooke cantered up unconcerned.

'Sorry,' he said, and emerged from his blazer in Achilles Club colours. Andrew glanced at his plain white things, longer and tighter than Redbrooke's.

The runners eyed each other as they took their places on the track. Redbrooke was a shade taller than Andrew and perfectly formed. His corn-coloured hair was a dishevelled crop, paler in hue than the tan of his face. His limbs flashed with youth and strength. His poise was quick as flame.

No wonder he can run, thought Andrew. He must win.

'I shall say on your marks—set—and then fire.'

At last, thought Andrew. His heart was beating in his throat now.

A second toiled by.

Andrew dropped to his knee for a sprinting start.

'Set!'

His knee quivered up from the track. It was toes and knuckles now, a balance quivering with tautness.

CRASH.

Scurry. Shoulders jostling. Mind out.

Andrew shot clear, going at top speed. He swung into the inside place. So far, so good. He'd got his inside place, and the lead too. Was he to make the running? He settled down into a stride, fast but easy.

He breathed calmly through his nose. Although the race had started, he still felt very nervous—an exhilarating nervousness now. He saw each blade of grass where cut turf edge met track. A groundsman set down a whitewash pail.

Andrew realized he was cutting out too fast a pace. He swung into a slower stride. So far all had gone according to plan, and he began to take courage.

As they approached the pavilion for the first time and the second long corner of the race, he found Perry was creeping up on his outside. Andrew was surprised and a little worried. In all the half-miles he had run before the pace he had set would have assured him the lead. He decided to make no effort, and Perry passed stride by stride and dropped into the lead. Andrew continued at his own pace, and a gap of a yard or two opened.

As they came on to the bend there was a sudden

sputter of feet and Andrew found that Brewster had
filled the gap.   Others were coming up, and he
realized that the whole field was moving faster than
he was.   He quickened up slightly and swung out
tentatively to pass Brewster again.   Before he could
pass the corner was reached.   He at least knew better
than to run on the outside round the curve; so he
slackened again to pull back into the inside.   But in
the very thought of doing so, the runner behind closed
smoothly and swiftly up to Brewster, and Andrew saw
that Redbrooke had got his inside berth.   Andrew had
to take the curve on the outside.   'Blinking fool,' he
told himself.

Old Jones and one or two other experienced runners
in the crowd caught each other's eyes for a moment;
the rest of the audience had no notion of the little
display of bad technique that Andrew had given.

So they went round the long curve.   Perry in the
lead and still pressing the pace;   Brewster second,
with no clear notion of what the pace ought to be,
and determined not to lose Perry;   Redbrooke
keeping wisely within striking distance and Andrew
bunched uncomfortably on the outside of Redbrooke
with two others.

By the time they came out of the long bend and
completed the first half of the race, Andrew was
thoroughly rattled.   Never had he felt such a strain
at this stage of a half-mile.   Already it was difficult
to get enough air;   he was no longer breathing evenly
through his nose.   Already a numbing weakness was
creeping down the front of his thighs.   Hopeless now
to think of gaining ground.   With relief he found he

was able to drop into the inside again behind Redbrooke. They had been running now for about one-
minute—it seemed an age. Could he possibly stick to it
for another period, as long again? The long stretch
of straight in front of him, the long sweep of curve at
the end of the ground that only brought you at the
beginning of the finishing straight. Then the sprint.
Already he felt he could not find an ounce of sprint.

Pace by pace he stuck to it, watching Redbrooke's
feet.

But even now he must quicken up if he was to hold
Redbrooke. At each step Redbrooke's back was
leaving him. He struggled to lengthen, but it was
useless. Redbrooke was moving up to the front.
Now he was equal with Brewster; now with Perry;
now he was in the lead. How easy Redbrooke's move
down the back-straight looked from the grandstand.
'Pretty running,' people told each other. 'Just the
place to come up.' 'Nicely judged.' 'See how he
worked himself through from the last corner.'

And this was the very place at which Andrew had
meant to move up himself. He remembered nothing
of his plans now. It was impossible to increase his
effort. One of the men behind came smoothly by and
dropped into the gap that Redbrooke had left in front
of him. The sixth man came up on his outside. There
was a kind of emptiness at his back. He was running
equal last.

Now they came to the final curve before the
finishing straight. His legs seemed powerless. He
grunted for breath. The weakness in his thighs had
grown to a cramping pain. And all the time with

full despair he saw Redbrooke going up, now five yards clear, now eight. Perry had dropped back to third, and Brewster was chasing Redbrooke.

Dark waves of pain swept over Andrew. Hopeless. Hopeless.

Still he must keep running with control. He must force his legs to a smooth long stride. This was the worst part of any race.

'Come on,' he told himself, 'another fifty yards —guts, man—guts.'

Had only Andrew known what the others were feeling, he would have taken courage. The whole pace of the first quarter, thanks to Andrew's own excitement, had been faster than anyone cared for. Redbrooke, untrained as he was, had found himself badly winded at the quarter-mile mark. He, too, doubted whether he would have any punch left at the finish. He determined, therefore, to make a surprise effort early when he still had a powerful sprint in him. As soon as they came into the curve, he stepped on the gas as hard as he could, three hundred yards from home, and steamed away. He jumped a lead of five, eight, ten yards before Perry or Brewster realized what was happening. It was a thing the crowd could follow better than the men in the race.

Now as they came into the straight, Andrew thought Redbrooke was gathering himself for a final dash. Far from it; he was hanging on for grim death. His sparkling effort had died right away. His stride was nerveless. The sprinting muscles in his thighs had lost every ounce of their power. He was struggling and asking himself at every stride: 'Can I,

4   (H 206)

can I, can I—surely those steps are drawing nearer—can I last it?'

Perry was desperately run out. Brewster had already been chasing Redbrooke hard for the last thirty yards, but could not find any pace at all.

Andrew alone of the field had he known it had been nursing his remnant of strength round that gruelling bend. Only forty yards to go now and he could throw all he had into a last desperate effort. Keep it up just a moment more. Thirty yards to the straight now—twenty—suddenly his control was shattered. He was fighting in a mindless fury of effort for every ounce of strength in him.

In ten yards he saw his whole fortune in the race change. He *had* got a sprint, then! The man on his outside vanished. He raced round the outside of the fellow in front hand over fist as he came into the straight. In another few yards he had the faltering Perry taped.

He had already run into third place. New strength surged through his limbs. 'Come on, come on: up, you can catch Brewster. Level. Feel him struggling. He can't hold you. Got him!'

Far, far off, a distant frenzied pain, somewhere; someone else's pain. Miles away a face on the side of the track.

Second now. Second, and he could catch Redbrooke. But could he catch him in time? They were past the start of the hundred yards now: a bare hundred to go. Could he? Could he? The first brilliance of his sprint had gone. He was fighting again in an agonising weakness that dragged his legs back.

But he was doing it, foot by foot. Fists clenched, to force speed-spent muscles.

Split seconds dragged strange length out. The straight went on and on. Five yards behind, now four, now three.

Redbrooke heard him, then felt him: two yards behind, now at his shoulder. He racked himself for a new effort. Together they swept past the hundred-yards finish, ten yards from the half-mile tape, with the dull roar of the crowd in their ears. Redbrooke saw he was beaten, but stuck to it till the last foot.

Then Andrew led.

A splendour of gladness as he watched the stretch of white wool break on his own chest.

'You've done it, you've done it!' Incredible precious moment.

Then he dropped half-unconscious on the track.

Strong arms plucked him up and walked him to the grass.

'Well done, very fine finish,' he heard. Down again, sitting now. The world swam round you. There was Redbrooke, standing up—not so done, then.

Ache, how those legs ache, and your thigh muscles too—must stand up. Hell, what does it matter, though, when you won!

Redbrooke came over to Andrew, smiling and controlled.

'Well done,' he said, 'you had me nicely.'

'Ow,' said Andrew, still panting, 'muscles in my thighs.' He got up and limped about. His legs felt absurd. The muscles in his haunches hurt abominably.

Redbrooke smiled. 'I know that feeling,' he said, 'comes of running untrained.'

'Oh, I had trained a bit,' said Andrew, 'a fair amount really. Do you know what the time was?'

'One-fifty-nine and two-fifths,' Redbrooke told him. 'I was just inside two minutes. I must say I think we did fairly well for the first effort of the season.'

'One-fifty-nine and two-fifths,' said Andrew, 'was it really?'

One of the judges joined them.

Others came up. They all said the same.

'Why on earth didn't you sprint before?'

'No idea I could,' explained Andrew.

Brewster joined the group.

'Well, that's my last half-mile,' he said. 'Never had to move so fast in my life before.'

But he was obviously pleased. He had finished about ten yards behind Redbrooke and must have done about two-two to two-three.

Now Andrew began to enjoy himself thoroughly. Gloriously relaxed in mind and body, gloriously contented, he watched the other events. He made new friends. Then he went in and soaked himself in a steaming bath and smoked, shouting to Brewster in the next compartment. Life was very kind.

He came out on to the ground, chatted with everyone he saw: discussed his race a dozen times: had three or four beers: spent a few shillings with extravagance. He saw, to his amazement, Redbrooke turn out again for the quarter and fight another gruelling finish to win by inches in fifty-one and a fifth seconds. Andrew was the first to pat him on the back.

'Great work,' he said.   'How you managed it after that half beats me!'

'Oh, well,' said Redbrooke, 'it loosened me up. Why didn't you come, lazy devil?'

In the bus going home, Andrew leant back and puffed deeply at his pipe. Alone for the first time, he went over the race in his mind. Well, he had done it. He could tackle anything on earth now.

After all, running was a thing men had always done. Football, other games, came and went. A good runner was a good runner for all time—with hundreds and hundreds of years of kinship behind him. And he, Andrew, was a good runner. A class runner. One-fifty-nine. Damn good!

His head was slightly swimming with fatigue and excitement and beer. He leant back and sighed—as happy as it is possible to be on this planet.

PHYLLIS BOTTOME

CAESAR'S WIFE'S EAR

Phyllis Bottome was born in Kent in 1882. *Her father was American, but her mother was English and she has retained her British nationality. After spending her early childhood in England, she was later educated in America. She wanted to be an actress, but she was obliged to abandon her hopes when she was attacked by tuberculosis. She went to Davos in Switzerland to be cured, and spent the next thirty years living and working in Switzerland, France, Austria and Italy. During the First World War she married, and when her husband was working in Vienna in the post-war period of ruin and famine there, she organized relief for the starving Austrians. Later she and her husband lived in Tyrol and Italy. Her intimate knowledge of Central Europe helped to provide the authentic atmosphere of several of her novels. She early became aware of the threat to her ideas and ideals foreshadowed by the rise of Nazism and Fascism, and her best-known novel,* The Mortal Storm (1937), *was an exposure of the workings of the Nazi regime. It was later made into a successful film.*

Her husband, Mr. A. E. Forbes Dennis, is a psychologist, and her own deep interest in psychology (especially in the work of Adler, on whom she wrote Alfred Adler: Apostle of Freedom) *is to be seen in many of her novels. Its influence is very evident in the story printed here. Mr. and Mrs. Forbes Dennis now live in Kensington.*

Phyllis Bottome's recreations are reading, conversation and travel. She wrote her first novel when she was only seventeen. Her reputation as a novelist and short story writer was first established in America, but her books have since had a wide sale in her own country and have been translated into many European languages. She believes that the basis of good fiction is a good story, but she has said: 'If an author is true to his characters they will give him his plot.'

●

Seppel Bergener did not find it altogether easy to be a good American.

He was born ten miles from Budapest; dimly in the overgrown jungle of his restless mind he could still remember that wide yellow worm, the Danube, on whose treacherous, marshy banks he had spent the first three years of his life.

Sometimes when he was drunk there spluttered in his ears the dazzling fireworks of z's and s's which comprised his native tongue. He could not have spoken Hungarian; but had anyone spoken it to him, his blood would have answered. As it was, Seppel spoke a clipped, fumbling American; and when he listened to the strange, flat language now always in his ears, he had to make those piteous efforts to hear made by the deaf in danger.

Seppel lived in the heart of a Californian desert. All day long the hot, clean wind whipped his senses.

His mother was dry and bright like a flame. She

was a Hungarian gipsy. Some people said she had
killed her husband. Others said that the lions had
killed him. Seppel's parents bred and trained lions
for show.

The police had come out into the desert to investi-
gate the sudden death of Seppel's father. His body
had been savaged by the lions, but the lions evaded
the third degree and the police could not persuade
them to 'come clean'. The police had the idea that
Seppel's father might have been killed first, and then
thrown to the beasts. But again the lions foiled them,
for they had made the evidence quite inconclusive.

Seppel was five years old at the time; he did not
care very much about his father's death. He loved his
mother and he loved the lions. He did not love a
young step-father, who was their showman, and who
took control of the show shortly after Seppel's father
died.

Seppel grew up fast, and took his education as it
was forced upon him. A huge grizzly bear caught him
once and hugged one shoulder out of shape. A
panther clawed his chin, and left very little of it.
Seppel played with lion and tiger cubs as if they were
his human contemporaries, and the marks of his little
play-fellows stood out all over his compact, small
body.

Seppel never grew to be a tall man, but he was very
vigorous and had eyes as clear as flame.

On his sixteenth birthday his mother said to him:
'You lion-man now! You mak' lions like dogs! You
great little son of mine! You hav' my heart an' my
blood! You no mak' showman ever, you no hav'

beauty. Pity! But for one maker of lions, there is plenty showmen! Aah! a-plenty!'

His mother must have known what she was talking about, because she had five showmen husbands, one after the other. The last of the five was still living when she died. But she left him nothing. She left every lion, bear, cat and cub to her son Seppel. The whole show—cages; cars; the shack and tents; the hot dog and iced-beer stands—was now Seppel's.

There was no dispute about it either, for Seppel's mother had made her will in Los Angeles itself, assisted by a famous lawyer. It was deposited in the city safe and published in the newspapers. In Caterina Sybylla's life there had been 'plenty showmen' but only one son.

Seppel was twenty-three when his mother died. He got rid of his showman step-father at once, and married a desert girl, with dry crinkly hair and a voice like the cracked shriek of a desert wind. Her teeth were bad; but she spoke good American.

'You faithful,' Seppel explained to her, 'I—kind! You once like other feller—you die! Same as my father feeded by lions. You 'member? I must have showman—see? You better no look at him! Pity if you look at him!'

Carrie Gladys replied raspingly with a string of oaths directed at showmen. She would not look at show-men, she averred, not if Rudolph Valentino[1] or Doug. Fairbanks[2] headed the list. Carrie Gladys was not an affectionate woman. She never noticed what anybody else felt about anything, unless she was personally involved. Her real passions were for gin and horses, and she knew that Seppel could give her plenty of both.

For a year after their marriage Seppel tried to do without a showman. He trained and showed his lions single-handed; but the Picture people told him that he was too small and unimpressive-looking to draw a big public and that they could not use him for films. So Seppel set to work to find a suitable showman, without too much charm.

Bert Kimstock was no Valentino; but he was six feet tall, with curly, brown hair, the bright eyes of a native Irishman, a long upper lip, nerve, and no money. Seppel engaged him reluctantly after two or three hours spent with Bert in the cages of the easier lions.

Seppel explained carefully to the new showman how he ran his show. 'This I do,' he told him; 'I mak' lions easy! I mak' 'em tricks! They're my baby boys! I no hav' children. I hav' lions! You—you can hav' children! An' you can play with my lions— once I mak' 'em easy! I show you how to be safe: you stan' in the big cage where people come—see? I mak' tricks an' you look good! The lions no hurt you! But the lions are mine! You un'erstan' you just showman? I—lion man!'

Bert assented heartily. He did not want to be a lion man. He was not without a genuine love and know-ledge of animals; he even possessed an old tame lioness called Pansy Bell, whom Seppel allowed him to bring into the show; and with Seppel's help he half-tamed a lioness cub called Rosamund—but Bert only half-tamed her. Rosamund had heaps of fun wrestling with

Bert in her cage—but there were moments when it looked as if she would have thought it still greater fun to have killed him; and with the male lions Bert had no success whatever.

Lions, however well trained, are never so madly affectionate as lionesses; and Seppel's lions were one-man animals, and refused to extend their patronage to Bert.

Seppel's favourite lion was called Caesar. He was the best trick lion the show had ever possessed. He had a huge brown mane, sleepy yellow eyes, and when he roared, he set the desert quivering.

Seppel told Bert confidentially, 'Caesar's safe as houses; houses where no fire comes. Mustn't bring fire near desert houses. No! No! Mustn't bring flame near lions either! Flame to lions, all same flame to mens. Woman—she flame! You understan'— never come between a lion and a lioness—then lions no safe—they kill—all same men in desert!'

Bert saw this point too; and thought that it did not concern him. He had already seen Carrie Gladys and he did not look on her in the light of a flame. Bert was an honest, rather boastful young man without intensity. He soon found that he was quite unable to teach lions tricks. He had not begun young enough nor did he possess the wild hypnotic eye-language and deep creative patience with which Seppel was endowed both by birth and training. Still the audience gave Bert their chief applause, and all he had to do to win it was to stand once a day in the big arena cage and take picturesque attitudes, while Seppel kept the male lions in their proper places.

The animals, let out of their cages by slip-gates, came through a subterranean passage one by one into the big main cage. The lionesses came first; and as they came in Seppel called them each by name to take their places. Their perches were arranged in a ring round the arena, the first seven feet from the ground, the others gradually rising in height to nine feet. The lionesses took the first perch from the top of a tub; and then sprang from perch to perch. It was Bert's business to face the lionesses, after they were seated, gluing them to their seats with his eyes and flicking them with a whip, if this reminder should be necessary. Venus was the last of the ladies upon the right, Mariposa the last upon the left.

Mariposa was the wife of Caesar. She was above suspicion[3] in every sense of the word; and even if she had not been, Caesar would have kept her so.

Venus had the worst temper of all the lionesses, but she was deeply attached to Seppel, who had helped her on one occasion to rear her cubs, when her natural milk supply had given out. Venus looked upon Seppel as a woman and a sister, and treated him accordingly. But as far as other males were concerned, including all lions, she had what is known in psychiatric circles as 'a strong masculine protest' and she took every occasion of showing it. She hunched herself up, and spat at the male lions as they entered, and if one of them came within striking distance of her, Venus promptly clawed him.

After the lionesses were seated, Seppel called for the young males. These were not powerful or excitable lions. They sat on tubs beneath the ladies' perches, looking a little bored; and the ladies looked well over their heads, towards the hatchway door.

Seppel then called to the attendants; 'Bring in my baby-boys!' Seppel's 'baby-boys' were full grown; and the most powerful male lions in the show. When they opened their jaws, if it was only to yawn, their teeth looked like the worst rocks a ship ever split on. If they roared, the cage rocked. Caesar always led them in, and then took his place at the end of the line, farthest from the hatchway, under the perch of Venus. This was intentional because Seppel trusted Caesar the most, and so great was Caesar's faithfulness to Mariposa that he never increased the masculine protest of Venus by so much as a glance.

Mariposa sat on the perch farthest from Caesar, but she always watched him with her fond lazy yellow eyes.

When the first trick was over, Bert would turn, and stand picturesquely in the centre of any pattern which Seppel had devised. Nobody noticed Seppel very much, except the big male lions whose eyes he always held.

Caesar and Mariposa shared a large cage next to that of a handsome male tiger, the only mature tiger possessed by the show. His name was Hector[4] and his manners were regrettably Trojan. His mate having been temporarily removed from his society to attend to her maternal duties, Hector became highly envious of the placid domesticity enjoyed by his neighbours. One morning he jumped much higher than he was supposed to be able to jump against the wooden partition, and tore off a large piece of steel netting which separated the two cages, as if it were sponge cake. He then proceeded to seize Mariposa's ear; and tore that.

Everyone thought there was an earthquake from the noise that followed; and Mariposa thought that she was the earthquake.

More and more tiger got through the steel netting, and Caesar, shaking the desert with his voice, skilfully seized Mariposa by the haunches, and dragged her clear of the tiger, minus half an ear. He then flung himself against the wooden partition and clawed down more netting, in order to get a stronger hold on Hector. By this time Seppel, Bert and two terrified attendants were gathered about the cages.

A glance was enough to show Seppel what had occurred. Half of Mariposa's ear was in the tiger's cage—and a good deal of tiger was being clawed by Caesar. The partition bulged like a piece of sailcloth caught in a breeze.

It grieved Seppel to interfere with Caesar, but he could not afford the death of his only tiger. He therefore entered Hector's cage from the rear and strikingly diverted his attention. Hector turned on him in a flash; but quicker still, Seppel covered the tiger's head with an enormous sack, and with the nervous help of Bert and the attendants, transferred Hector to a distant cage.

Mariposa yelped for hours, while Caesar lay beside her, licking her torn ear, and administering consolation in low throaty growls.

In the course of a few days Mariposa, except for half an ear, completely recovered. Caesar's temper, however, was desperately ruffled; nor could he ever

again feel the same trust in Seppel. 'That one lil' tiger!'
Seppel told him persuasively, 'he no more trouble
any lion! He flat skin to walk on—sure enough dead!
My wife she step on him in kitchen!' Caesar blinked
disdainfully at this tale for cubs. Did he not know the
voice of every creature in the show, and was he likely
to forget the still audible roar of a tiger that had
trifled with Mariposa's ear?

Seppel excused Caesar from the ring for two weeks,
though it was both difficult and dangerous to get on
without him. At last he said to Bert, 'My big baby-
boy, he come back today. He lead once more. There
may be lil' trouble! You look lionesses hard; and
if tub fall over—you pick up tub pretty quick; better
tub no fall over! Better lionesses come in lil' bit
slow—and the young lions lil' bit quick!' Bert agreed,
but he did not feel too comfortable. One lioness is
one thing, but somehow or other ten lionesses are a
good deal more than ten things.

However, the lionesses made a good entry. Venus
took some time to settle; but Mariposa leapt to her
usual perch like a bird. The young lions were hurried
in, to get them out of the way; and then the big male
lions, led by Caesar, came in very slowly, and with
great dignity. Seppel's flying, intensely beseeching
eyes met Caesar's. Caesar turned his heavy head away,
but after a moment's perceptible pause, he obeyed
Seppel's pleading will, and took his seat on his tub.
The other lions all mounted theirs in turn, while
Seppel's earnest, plangent voice told them what good
boys they were! What handsome children! What
grand lions!

The lionesses remained on their perches, bored,
but quiescent. The young males, resentfully expectant,
watched their fathers advance slowly, facing Seppel,
one by one. Each in his turn; each taking his exact
place; following Seppel's high-keyed, imploring
voice, his summoning eyes, and the direction of the
whiplash, that without touching them showed each
his place and warned him to take it.

Unfortunately Caesar declined. He stood at the
end of the row, in his accustomed place; but lie down
he would not. He snarled; he raised a paw; he
lashed an angry yellow tail. His massive benevolent
upper lip turned hideous with menace.

Mariposa, watching him intently from her perch,
grew larger while she watched.

Seppel beseeched; he coaxed; he flung his heart
out at Caesar: his boy—his baby-boy! Surely to
please him Caesar *would* lie down?

The whip flickered and flapped in front of Caesar's
face. Caesar put his paw on it. He bit it; and
wouldn't lie down. He even jerked back a pace or
two, nearer Venus's perch. Venus snarled savagely—
and in her ill-natured prudery, she clawed at the
flank of the lady next to her. Dolores—the lady next
to her—swayed, lost her balance and fell into the
arena.

Seppel glided away from his big males. He got
behind Dolores, who was slinking, perchless and
nervous, round the ring, and whipped her up on to a
tub. Dolores leapt; missed her footing; and the tub
rolled over.

Bert had an uncomfortable feeling that he ought to

do something about that fallen tub; but with nine lionesses staring at him—and Mariposa swollen out of all recognition—he knew that turning his back on them, to right the tub, would be a most unpleasant posture.

Seppel gave a whimpering cry like a frightened child. 'Will no-one helpa me?' he cried. 'Will I be all alone for ever—no-one to helpa—me?' But while he whined and whimpered, he deftly righted the tub; lashed Dolores on to it, and saw her successfully negotiate her perch, before turning back with a bound, to face his baby-boys.

The lions had broken up their row. They stood on the balls of their feet, tense and terrible.

Seppel ran close up to them, calling each by name, meeting their fierce yellow eyes with the quick flame of his own. 'Caesar!' he called. 'Pompey! Tomboy! Kaiser! Capone! Paasha! Ajax! Lindbergh! Duce! Poppa! There you go! Easy my fine boys—you lie down! You good boys! You, Caesar! You my pet boy! Oh Kay! Oh Kay! O.K. lions!' One by one they sank back, down on their haunches; into their statuesque row. Only Caesar still stood upright, lashing his tail with disdainful puckered lips. Seppel's voice cajoled on. His will burned through his eyes. At last Caesar's head sank; his beautiful lithe flanks closed in. He lay down at the end of his row. Mariposa grew slowly smaller again.

The hatch door reopened, and the lions filed out in turn.

Then Seppel faced Bert in the empty cage, while the audience still applauded.

He called out in his fierce high voice: 'Why you no helpa me, showman? Why you stan' there—you great ape? You fat stuck pig! You no helpa me put tub straight! I say one momen' more, one li' instan' all those lions go wild! Go mad! We get feeded by lions! I no can nothing save! I hold 'em with my eyes! I turn my back they loose—they no hold! They go pieces! They no more my children! You no un'erstan'! You only showman. Oh, my God! Only showman! One day all dead for nothing! And my poor baby-boys all shotted up and cursed! An' all your fault! You stupid—you God-damn stupid showman!' and Seppel tore open the cage door and ran sobbing, through the astonished audience to find his wife.

Some women would have comforted Seppel and taken the bitterness out of his heart, by their fears for his safety; but Carrie Gladys was no comforter. Her ideal was a cave man; and she did not know that courage can be fed by tears.

Behind Seppel stood Bert; tall, handsome and cheerfully explanatory. It was all right! The Boss had had an upset! Not an animal damaged, though—and a good audience! Plenty of money!

Carrie Gladys took Bert's explanations down like gin. She said derisively to Seppel: 'Go on—and get in there—cry-baby!' She said to Bert: 'Have a drink!' They had a drink and Carrie Gladys laughed. She may not have laughed at her husband; but he heard her laugh. Carrie Gladys had a good deal to learn from lionesses.

Night fell. Towards morning a lion roared. His

hollow, hungry voice shattered the desert stillness into harsh, dry flakes of sound.

Seppel lay awake, brooding and resentful, by his wife's side. 'My boy—my baby-boy!' he whispered to himself. He knew it was Caesar roaring. Caesar was roaring because he felt defeated. Hector was still alive; and Caesar had obeyed Seppel—who was no longer to be trusted, since he kept Hector alive.

Seppel, too, felt defeated. He had cried; and Carrie Gladys had laughed at him with his showman.

The morning broke hotter than the day before. The desert wind came in long burning puffs as if the earth had opened a secret chimney and was sighing out fire.

Mariposa and Venus, who were lying side by side on a rock in the middle of the yard, looked as if they were made of the same yellow stone that they were lying on. Nothing moved about them except their tawny eyes. The mountains hung like jagged sheets of cardboard against a brazen sky.

There was an ominous rasping quality in the day. Men's tempers were short and uncertain. The animals were inert and unresponsive. Even the tiger cubs were less playful than usual. They bit and scratched mechanically and fell asleep while doing it.

Seppel went the round of the cages muttering to himself. The polar bear lay prostrate in his pool, with only the top of his head and one irritated red eye showing. The monkeys were beating their wives and the wives were screaming like mad. Seppel watched them for a time, but thought there was not much harm being done, and that it would be a pity to interfere with a male prerogative.

At last he came to Caesar's cage. Caesar was in a very low frame of mind. He refused even to come forward and speak to Seppel.

Seppel pleaded for a long time with Caesar; but Caesar only sat on his haunches and blinked. Once, he even put his paw on the bars, and shook them.

Seppel took this very much to heart; but Bert, standing good-naturedly beside him, thought the whole affair rather a joke. 'You no un'erstan' lions,' Seppel said bitterly. 'They gotta strong feelin's, lions! They no get over things! Once you hurt a lion—you hurt a heart!'

'Well—what you goin' ter do about it?' Bert asked him; 'if Caesar's so damn hurt—how you going ter manage? Goin' ter give another lion the lead? Caesar held you up yesterday! And ter-day's Sunday! We'll have a swell audience, maybe! They won't want ter wait half an hour, while you baby Caesar into lying down, will they?'

Seppel shook his head gloomily. 'Caesar my stunt lion,' he said sadly. 'I no give up my stunt lion! Not for no Sunday audience! No! Caesar *mus'* come in! Only today I feed him myself—*first* I mak' him more fren'ly. I talk him alone! She very fine lioness, Caesar's wife—she better'n a woman! But half an ear—that not enough to break a show down! No, sir. Caesar—he learn understan' 'bout his wife's ear!'

It was stupid of Bert to neglect Seppel's instructions. He forgot to tell the attendants not to feed Caesar with the other lions. When Seppel came from his

Sunday dinner, with a handsome meal for Caesar, it was to find that he had been already fed; nor did Bert attach any very great importance to Seppel's sudden burst of maniacal rage, when he found that he was too late to feed his pet. Like Carrie Gladys, Bert was untroubled by the feelings of others. He was a good-natured fellow, accustomed to getting his own way; and winning applause for it.

Still, he went so far as to suggest that perhaps it would be better for Caesar to remain in his cage and not take the lead in the afternoon performance. Seppel, who was just about to give this order, immediately reversed it, and told the attendant to let Caesar start the line of male lions as usual.

There was a large Sunday audience. The animals came in nicely and without confusion.

The first two tricks ran as smooth as cream.

Bert had a fine easy wrestling match with his pet lioness. Pansy Bell gave him a showy struggle and never forgot herself for a moment. When she withdrew, Bert stood every inch a lion-tamer in front of his circle of lionesses, while Seppel inconspicuously in the back of the cage engaged the attention of the male lions.

Suddenly a blanched darkness swept over the faces of the audience. It was like a cloud crossing the sun. Bert saw rows of mouths open suddenly and eyes pricked wide with horror. Something had happened behind him, which he could not see.

Caesar had suddenly decided that if he couldn't kill Hector, the nearest male lion might do instead.

With one bound he had launched himself on Poppa

and torn half his flank open. All the lions grew tense and crouched for a charge. Seppel stood alone in the middle of a ring of lions—calling—calling.

Bert looked behind him. There was just one chance in a million. Anything he did might tell now. A sudden noise might hold the lions. If he jumped through the ring and stood by Seppel, there might be a chance for their lives. A moment later, nothing could stop the lions from charging. Bert stood close to the hatchways. Once inside them he would be safe. Venus chose that moment of his conflict to leap down from her perch. The chance was over. Bert jumped for the hatchway. A terrific roar crashed behind him. He ran through the smelly passage, hot and flurried, asking himself over and over again how he could have saved Seppel.

The first cage door closed safely behind him. He was free now. He reminded himself that Seppel too had a door at his back. If Seppel broke through the ring of lions—if he risked the danger to the audience by opening the cage door that faced them—if that roar had not meant the lions were already on him—then perhaps he was safe!

The whole, hot empty yard rocked with sound. Bert found a gun, and ran through the yard towards the arena cage. It would look more like a rescue than an escape if he came back with a gun.

As he came within sight of the cage, he heard high above the pulverizing roar of the lions Seppel's voice, shrill—plangent—strained but curiously without fear or anger. 'My boys! My baby-boys! Caesar! Poppa! Paasha!' Seppel was calling them still. He was down under them; but they hadn't quite killed him.

The terror-stricken audience pushed each other aside, to let Bert through. He steadied his gun against the steel rims of the cage, and shot Caesar through the heart. With a roar that drowned the shrieks of the crowd and the clamour of the other animals, Mariposa flung herself from her perch on to the body of Caesar.

The rest of the lions drew back, crouched and growling; but it was not Bert's shot that controlled them. It was Seppel's voice; he lay in the centre of the ring, incredibly mauled, a mere mask of blood.

'Back—back, my beauties!' he cried beseechingly, and then one by one he called their names.

The attendant opened the hatchway door. The lions withdrew sullenly, but in their usual order. The lionesses left their perches.

Mariposa never moved, nor after that one roar, did she make a sound. She lay across the body of Caesar so still that you could not tell which of them was dead.

Venus, too, refused to follow her sisters. She leapt from her perch, and crouched, swaying, across the bloody floor to Seppel's side. 'God! she'll finish him!' shrieked Carrie Gladys, her white papery face pressed against the bars; but she was judging Venus by her own standard.

'Is that Venus? Is that my darling?' Seppel called faintly. The lioness crouched low beside him—and with a sigh Seppel leaned his bleeding head against her flank. She licked his wounds with low caressing growls, nor would she let anyone approach him, until she knew that he was safely dead.

Notes

1. *Rudolph Valentino*: (*d.* 1926), was a film actor much admired by women in 'handsome lover' parts.
2. *Douglas Fairbanks*: (*d.* 1939), was famous in films for his playing of dashing, athletic heroes, as in *The Three Musketeers*.
3. *She was above suspicion*: this is an allusion to the saying of Julius Caesar, 'Caesar's wife must be above suspicion'.
4. *Hector . . . Trojan*: Hector was, of course, a Trojan hero but it was not he, but his brother Paris, who ran off with another man's wife.

THE PRODIGAL CALF

John Brophy was born in Liverpool in 1899, and educated at Holt School. In 1914 he ran away from school, shortly before his fifteenth birthday, and enlisted in the King's Regiment, with which he served as a private soldier in France and Belgium. Later he studied at the Universities of Liverpool and Durham and taught for two years in Egypt. After that he worked in a general store, writing novels in the evenings. Since then he has written over thirty novels, some of which have been filmed.

●

This happened in Italy in the mountains.

One night a small squad of infantrymen was ordered to move forward and establish a post just behind the crest of a tiny hill between two other hills, themselves only the lower buttresses of a hill so big that it was often referred to as 'the mountain'. The Germans held part of 'the mountain': a few days before they had held all of it. The squad was led by Corporal Basham, and when he set off he had five men.

The food was sufficient to last forty-eight hours. After that, if they were not relieved, the squad would have their emergency rations to fall back on.

On the way forward two of the squad were hit by a

shell which burst on a rock. One man got a piece of
splintered casing in his chest. The other came off
more lightly, and Corporal Basham ordered him to
lead the badly hit man back to an aid post. The
remainder of the party were now heavily burdened
with food, barbed wire, mines, and boxes of grenades
and ammunition, as well as their weapons and
equipment. They reached the little hill more than
half an hour after scheduled time.

It was after midnight now. Corporal Basham
surveyed his position and found a nick in the ground,
near the top of the ridge, where he could post a man
to watch forward. Then he arranged a roster for
guard duties and sited the two Bren guns. It looked
as though, only four in all, he and his men would get
little sleep, and he was glad that his outpost duty was
to last no more than forty-eight hours.

'The mountain' towered above him as he lay beside
his Bren gun. It shouldered up, black and massive,
against the stars. Posts, stronger than his own, were
to be established on the two buttress hills, and that
meant that he would be protected on both flanks.
But about an hour after the Corporal had completed
his arrangements, there came sudden abrupt noises,
first from the right flank, then from the left: sudden
spirts of golden light; muzzle flashes; pistol flares;
the crimson flamings of detonated grenades; the
rat-tat-tat of automatic fire, and shouts.

'Looks like they've run into Jerry out there,' said
Corporal Basham. He wondered if the flank posts
would be established after all. If not, the situation
would not be so funny. He reckoned to be pretty

tough himself, and he was glad the three men with him were tough types, also. The Corporal was a professional soldier. He was not tall but very strong, and he rather liked hard work: sweat and strain kept his self-respect in good condition. Of the other three, Gideon and Caleb were both townsmen, but neither of them soft-handed. Caleb had worked at a flour mill, on the hoists, before he joined the army, and Gideon's job was any sort of manual labour that came his way. He had worked with a shovel at coal depots, with a pneumatic drill at road-mending. And a dozen other jobs as well. The fourth man, Amos, was the only one who came from the country. He had worked on the same farm all his life, since he was a small boy, anyhow. Corporal Basham decided it would not have been easy to pick three likelier lads for the job in hand. They were tough, all right.

He moved up to where Gideon and Caleb were lying side by side. He found them cursing each other.

'What's up?' he whispered. 'And keep quiet, the pair of you.'

'Look at this, Corp.'

A small cylindrical ration can was thrust into his free hand.

'What's the matter with it?'

'It's milk,' Gideon whispered back.

'Well? What about it?'

'They're all milk. Caleb, the b.f., he must have picked up the wrong sack at the stores.'

'I tell you it was the Q.M.'s[1] fault,' Caleb protested. 'Anyhow, how could I tell the difference in the dark?'

'You ought to have made sure. You see what it is, Corp. We got biscuits and we got chocolate—fancy stuff. But no meat. No meat at all. Only about ten times as much milk as we want.'

'It wasn't my fault,' Caleb maintained.

'It was an' all.'

'Shut up, both of you!' said the Corporal. 'O.K. We've got milk instead of meat. Well it might have been worse. We just got to live on milk, that's all. It's nourishing, anyhow.'

     *   *   *   *   *   *   *

'Did you hear a sound just now?' Caleb asked the Corporal.

'Lots.'

'I don't mean that. I mean a funny sound. Like someone in pain. Or someone having a nightmare.'

'Where did it come from?'

'Couldn't tell. Listen! There it is again. It's not far away either.'

The sound was low, not strong, but strangely hollow and reverberant.

'You're right,' Corporal Basham whispered. 'It's not far away. But where? Keep your eyes skinned, both of you. I'm going back to warn Amos.'

This time he crawled over the rocks and the muddy grass, and when he came up beside Amos, before he could ask a question, Amos said, in his slow, deliberate way. 'Don't worry about that noise, Corp. I'll tell you what it is. It's a cow. That's all.'

'Sure?'

'Dead sure. Funny thing, though, it's behind us. It

might be a calf. Yes, it'll be a calf. Not a big one either.'

'I'm going to have a look,' said the Corporal.

Within ten minutes he brought them news. Amos had guessed right. The noises were made by a calf. The Corporal said he found it shut into a small enclosure of stone walls, which Amos said was probably a pen used when sheep were dipped. There was a brook running beside it. The calf was quite small, so far as the Corporal could see. The stone pen had been built in a hollow, with big boulders to protect it. There was no need now for them to dig a slit trench before daylight: all except the look-out man could go into the pen when daylight came.

'That calf,' said the Corporal, 'its head's not up to my waist.'

'Big enough,' Caleb decided. 'Now who says we've got no meat? And not bully either. Who's for a nice bit of fresh veal?'

They joked about the feasts they were going to have, and they argued about which parts of the meat they would roast and which they would boil.

'If the other lads knew what a bit of luck we're having,' said Gideon, 'they'd be volunteering by the dozen to come up here for dinner tomorrow.'

'That's right,' said Gideon. 'You don't want to cook meat as soon as it's killed. It ought to hang a bit.'

Soon after dawn, which came late, hindered by a heavy rainfall, the Corporal realized that the squad's position in the outpost was not so secure as it was designed to be. The platoons which had gone forward on the flanks to occupy the buttress hills in front had not been able to get there or, at any rate, to stay there. The Germans were in occupation. Gideon, moving clumsily, showed his head for a second or two over the sky-line, and at once bullets began to swish over and around the squad, some of them making silvery rapid arcs in the morning light as they ricochetted off rocks.

'Blast you, Gideon!' said the Corporal. 'Now they know we're here.'

But the Germans were not comfortable either. Their posts came under counter fire from British machine-guns and light artillery sited in the rear.

'Well,' said the Corporal. 'Jerry isn't going to come and disturb us here. Not with that field of fire to cross. We'll get by. It might be worse.'

'I'm hungry,' Gideon complained. 'A man wants meat. Biscuits and milk!'

'Well, what about that calf?'

Caleb said there was a hole in the ground where they could build a fire and do some cooking, and if one man stood by to beat the smoke away by flapping a coat, it wouldn't be detected on a drizzling, grey day. He was anxious to make amends for mistaking tins of milk for tins of preserved meat.

They left Gideon on guard and went back down the slope to look at the hole. Corporal Basham admitted that cooking was possible. He knew, too, that hot food on a day like this would make a lot of difference to the spirit of his men. So he told Amos to start a small fire and boil some water to make tea. Then, with Caleb, he went to look at the calf in the stone wall pen. It was making plenty of noise now.

In daylight it seemed very small. Its coat was

bedraggled with rain and mud. They could see its throat pulsating as it lowed at them.

'You know,' said Caleb, 'it'd look real nice, cleaned up a bit. Them reddish-brown patches on the white.'

'Don't talk sissy,' said the Corporal. 'What have you got to kill it with? Bayonet or your knife?'

'Kill it? Me? I wouldn't know how to begin. Tell you what, I'll slip back and help Amos brew up.'

The calf lowed again. It walked across to where they peered at it through a hole in the stone wall. Its eyes glistened, big and brown and lustrous, through the downpouring rain.

'And some people call themselves soldiers!'

'I'm not scared o' Jerry, Corporal. And anyhow, why don't you kill it yourself? It'd only need a short burst with your Sten gun.'

'Mustn't waste ammunition,' said Corporal Basham. 'Tell you what, we'll let Gideon do the job.'

'That's right. Gideon, he's the one. I remember he told me he used to work in a tannery once. It wouldn't mean anything to him.'

'All right,' the Corporal decided. 'You go and relieve him on guard. Tell him to report here at once.'

Gideon came back very cocky. Even though he had to crawl part of the way, and stoop when he was not crawling, he contrived to move with a swagger.

'Fancy Caleb turning soft like that,' he said. 'Don't you worry, though, Corp. I'll see to this.'

He unfastened the wicker gate and let himself into the pen. The calf came stumbling up to him at once.

He put out his hand and it nuzzled its lips against his palm.

Gideon looked up.

'It's no good,' he complained. 'I couldn't do it. I haven't the heart. I'd never sleep quiet again.'

The Corporal was almost beaten by this time. He had to remind himself that it was his duty to secure the best available provisions for his men in order to maintain maximum efficiency.

'It'll have to be Amos, then,' he declared.

'We ought to have thought of Amos first of all,' said Gideon. 'He's a farmer's boy. It won't mean anything to him.'

But Amos, when he was fetched to the pen, protested that he was no butcher. And as soon as he set eyes on the calf, he turned indignantly to the other two, completely disregarding the respect due to Corporal Basham's rank.

'You're a fine couple. Can't you see the poor beast's half-starved? Jerry drove away the cow, I expect, and forgot this poor little beggar. Just like Jerry!'

'Do you mean to say it's still taking milk?'

'Yes, and will be for months yet. Only I'll bet it's not had a feed for a couple of days. It wants its mother. It's weak, poor little blighter. It can hardly stand up. Haven't you got eyes in your heads?'

The Corporal felt as conscience-stricken as Gideon, till he had an idea.

'Of course,' he said, 'we've got lashings of milk.'

They made a run for the fire then, and opened a can of the condensed milk and mixed it with warm water in a mess tin. They fed the calf before they thought of feeding themselves. Amos dipped his fingers in the milk, and the calf sucked them. Then it began to lap from the mess tin, at first doubtfully and slowly, then fast.

As things turned out they had to stay quite a time in that outpost before the rest of the battalion worked forward on the flanks, and they could be relieved. They had to beat off several small attacks, too, and more than once they were shelled. But they all survived, including the calf.

When the squad at last marched out to rest, they were dirty and tired, dropping with sleep. They had lived for five days on two days' rations minus the essential meat, plus one day's emergency rations. Less than that, for most of the milk had gone to the calf. In effect, they had starved for the last forty-eight hours. Only the calf looked better for the experience. Its flanks were plumped out with tin after tin of milk, and the lowing noises it made were no longer plaintive, but full of the joy of life.

The squad was very proud of its acquisition. Next morning it discussed procedures for having the calf adopted as the regimental pet. But by afternoon an Italian farmer had visited the camp and claimed the calf as his property. After he had seen the interpreter and the interpreter had seen the adjutant, and several forms had been signed in triplicate, the farmer led the calf away in triumph.

'Well,' said Corporal Basham, 'that's that.'

'It's a bleedin' shame. We ought to have been allowed to keep it,' Caleb declared. 'It don't seem a bit fair somehow.'

6

Gideon also was not satisfied. 'I miss the little blighter,' he said. 'Tell you what, when the war's over, I'm coming back here somehow. Ship on a boat as a deckhand or something. And I'm going to look for that farmer, and tell him the least he can do is to give me a glass of milk. Free. For nix. And it's got to be milk from our calf. It'll be a fine cow by then, see.'

Amos laughed.

'You'll get no milk.'

'I will. Bet you I will. The old farmer chap won't grudge it me, when I tell him I saved his cow from certain death when it was a bit of a calf, hardly up to my waist.'

'You townies,' said Amos. 'You don't notice nothing. That was a bull calf.'

Note

1. *Q.M.*: quarter-master, the officer responsible for food supplies.

J. A. B. CUDDON

JUMPING FOR JOY

J. A. B. Cuddon was born in 1928 and was educated at Douai and at Brasenose College, Oxford. After reading for a degree in English he did two years' research for his B.Litt. on the Mediaeval and Renaissance conceptions of Satan. He has played first-class Rugby Football, and has worked as a professional cricket coach, schoolmaster and free-lance journalist. His special interest is the theatre and he has written a number of plays.

●

I have never yet been able to explain to myself how I was ever persuaded to do anything so foolhardy as to jump out of an aeroplane. I had no need of what is described rather sinisterly as 'danger money'; I did not greatly desire sensation; I am not given to bravado; I was not oppressed by unrequited love. But somehow I felt myself propelled to take the chance; some conspiracy of impulses had betrayed me, and for the first time I was about to do it and wondering what it was going to be like.

Now I know that jumping is rather like diving from an immense height into a large pool of cold water without any water in it. All the expected preliminary sensations and shock are present and, in a way, felt.

Then suspension comes and the body is reprieved. I am sure it reduces my life by years every time I do it, but for some reason I go on doing it.

With jellified knees, sanded mouth, hollow stomach, and the heart distempered by the urgent acceleration of a warning tattoo, I edged forward down the plane, making last-minute mental and equipment checks, and hooked up the static line which, like an umbilical cord,[1] joins the delivered body to the plane before ensuring its severance by releasing the 'chute. The roar of engines filled my ears; the door was open; the dispatcher ready; the red light flickered. . . .

Back on the training station preparations had been accompanied by an atmosphere of informality: that deceptive kind of informality which experts promote as a result of years of experience and professional certainty, but which in fact conceals great care and efficiency. There the instructors had treated 'jumping' as casually as they would an elementary domestic task. That in itself was both reassuring and exasperating. But now we were airborne things were different. The line of pale, preoccupied faces told how different. Occasionally someone shouted a forced jocularity to sustain his flagging spirits, but responses were polite and perfunctory. Each man had withdrawn into himself, and what was going on inside him was nobody's business.

Seen from below, the rapidity of ejection is surprising. The bodies spill and curve from the door like a squad of circus acrobats. Doing it is less artistic but a great deal more surprising.

As I shuffled forward to the opening I remembered what I had to do: knees drawn up, feet together, head tucked in. I stood at the edge of what seemed an appalling vacuity. The noise of the engines was shattering, but the silence of my mind and myself was more so. The air rushing past seemed almost visible and the earth beyond incredibly distant and immobile. I felt an acute sense of being ludicrous, but at the same time I was paralysed. Laughter was impossible. I should never have started this, I thought. I should have remained at my office desk, safe, comfortable, habitual. It was ridiculous to be jumping out of an aeroplane with only a large piece of silk to support me. Supposing it hadn't been packed properly? Supposing there was a flaw or a tear in it? Supposing it didn't come out? Or, if it did, supposing it didn't open? Or, supposing it opened, what if it shut again?

The possibilities raced through my brain. I had heard unpleasant accounts of people doing 'candles' when their ropes got twisted and the opening 'chute furled again and became a long, white-capped streamer or plume as the certain corpse hurtled to the ground. Already I saw it happening. I had heard macabre details of how high bodies bounced when they struck. Already it seemed to be happening to me. What a fool I had been, I thought. I was no Icarus,[2] no bird man; no land or sea would be named after me; merely another bald, terse note in the middle of the evening paper: 'There was an accident . . . his parachute failed to open . . . an inquiry will be made.'

If I had been sensible, I thought, I might at this moment be signing memoranda in my office in Mincing Lane[3] and thinking about my lunch at the 'local'. Then I thought of the miraculous escapes: people landing in reservoirs and snowdrifts and haystacks. It was absurd. I knew there weren't any reservoirs; there hadn't been any snow for three months and most of the haystacks were consumed by this time of the year. The seconds were ticking by. At any moment we would be over the dropping zone. I went on looking out of the door, hypnotized by my own fear, stiff and yet trembling. I knew I had to go. There was no turning back. Even at that stage my pride came to my rescue. It was any minute now. I ceased to think. My mind and body were paralysed by a total negation.

GO! My stomach seemed to fall out of me as I hit the slipstream[4] and was sucked away. Something rattled in my brain. I was certain it was the end; and, still mesmerized by my complete helplessness, the last vestiges of strength and purpose drained out of me as I began to plummet downwards. In the corner of one eye I saw the world, chequered, extraordinarily neat, roll beneath me. How absurd! How little! How enormous! And, what was more, I was going to hit it very shortly. Then, as I turned, I saw the plane in the corner of my other eye, at what seemed miles away, and the rest of the stick curving outwards. I was certain my 'chute wasn't going to open. It couldn't open. It hadn't opened. The cold air blasted through me and I was falling at a terrible speed. Then the first jerk went through my body. It was opening. I giggled and looked up. It was open, completely open. Then I looked down and felt sick. I still couldn't do anything. If the ropes twisted— they twisted. I had no more strength to do anything. The total abdication of will had allowed no successor.

Then suddenly I felt quite comfortable. The earth was not far away. It was coming up fast. The details on the ground were startlingly clear. I began to remember what I must do when I landed and how to land. For a second or two I felt wonderfully free, exhilarated, almost ecstatic. Then . . . down . . .rolling over . . . being dragged along . . . bang the release box. . . .

I scrambled to my feet and looked up and about. The others were landing. The pattern of normality began to rearrange itself. I trod the ground deliberately and felt ridiculously light-hearted. It had actually happened. How dull, I thought, to be in Mincing Lane signing memoranda, thinking about my lunch. And then I remembered that we had to do another jump the next day. Twenty-four hours to go. Twenty-four hours in which to—but I wasn't quite sure what. Perhaps it would be rather dull; but then there was always the chance that tomorrow the parachute wouldn't open.

Notes

1. *Umbilical cord*: the cord that joins the new-born animal to its mother.
2. *Icarus*: in Greek myth, he and his father Daedalus were the first men to fly, having wings fixed on with wax. There is a Greek island named after Icarus. The sea referred to is perhaps the Hellespont, named after

Helle, who was riding over it in the air on the back of
the ram with the Golden Fleece, when she fell off into
the water and was drowned.

3. *Mincing Lane*: a street in the City of London, well
known for its connection with the wholesale tea trade.

4. *Slipstream*: the turbulent air-current under and behind
an aircraft in flight.

C. S. FORESTER

THE EXAMINATION FOR LIEUTENANT

C. S. Forester (born in 1899) has written a number of popular and very competent novels, several of which have been filmed. They include The Ship, Brown on Resolution, The Gun, The African Queen *and a series of which the hero is Horatio Hornblower. Mr. Forester studied to be a doctor at Guy's Hospital, but failed to get a degree and turned to writing. At the early age of twenty-four he achieved success with his novel* Payment Deferred, *which proved so popular that it was turned into both a play and a film. During the Second World War the Ministry of Information encouraged him to go to sea in a British cruiser in the Mediterranean to collect material for his novel,* The Ship. *Later he made a similar voyage to the Bering Sea in an American warship; there he was unfortunately smitten by a disease that has turned him into a cripple, and forces him to live most of the year in California.*

Mr. Midshipman Hornblower, written in 1950 after the Hornblower novels had become very well known, takes us back to Hornblower's youth, and is a series of short stories about different episodes in his early years at sea. It is six or seven years before Trafalgar. Britain is at war with Napoleon's France and with Spain. When Acting-Lieutenant Horatio Hornblower sails into Gibraltar harbour on board H.M.S. Indefatigable *(commanded by Captain*

Pellew) *he is told that he must appear before a board to take his examination for lieutenant.*

●

H.M.S. *Indefatigable* was gliding into Gibraltar Bay, with Acting-Lieutenant Horatio Hornblower stiff and self-conscious on the quarterdeck beside Captain Pellew.[1] He kept his telescope trained over towards Algeciras; it was a strange situation, this, that major naval bases of two hostile powers should be no more than six miles apart, and while approaching the harbour it was as well to keep close watch on Algeciras, for there was always the possibility that a squadron of Spaniards might push out suddenly to pounce on an unwary frigate coming in.

'Eight ships—nine ships with their yards crossed, sir,' reported Hornblower.

'Thank you,' answered Pellew. 'Hands 'bout ship.'

The *Indefatigable* tacked and headed in toward the Mole. Gibraltar harbour was, as usual, crowded with shipping, for the whole naval effort of England in the Mediterranean was perforce based here. Pellew clewed up his topsails and put his helm over. Then the cable roared out and the *Indefatigable* swung at anchor.

'Call away my gig,[2]' ordered Pellew.

Pellew favoured dark blue and white as the colour scheme for his boat and its crew—dark blue shirts and white trousers for the men, with white hats with blue ribbons. The boat was of dark blue picked out with white; the oars had white looms and blue blades. The general effect was very smart indeed as the drive of the oars sent the gig skimming over the water to carry Pellew to pay his respects to the port admiral. It was not long after his return that a messenger came scurrying up to Hornblower.

'Captain's compliments, sir, and he'd like to see you in his cabin.'

'Examine your conscience well,' grinned Midshipman Bracegirdle. 'What crimes have you committed?'

'I wish I knew,' said Hornblower, quite genuinely.

It is always a nervous moment going in to see the captain in reply to his summons. Hornblower swallowed as he approached the cabin door, and had to brace himself a little to knock and enter. But there was nothing to be alarmed about; Pellew looked up with a smile from his desk.

'Ah, Mr. Hornblower, I hope you will consider this good news. There will be an examination for lieutenant tomorrow, in the *Santa Barbara* there. You are ready to take it, I hope?'

Hornblower was about to say 'I suppose so, sir,' but checked himself.

'Yes, sir,' he said—Pellew hated slipshod answers.

'Very well, then. You report here at three p.m. with your certificates and journals.'

'Aye aye, sir.'

That was a very brief conversation for such an important subject. Hornblower had Pellew's order as acting-lieutenant for two months now. Tomorrow he would take his examination. If he should pass, the admiral would confirm the order next day, and

Hornblower would be a lieutenant with two months'
seniority already. But if he should fail! That would
mean he had been found unfit for lieutenant's rank.
He would revert to midshipman, the two months'
seniority would be lost, and it would be six months
at least before he could try again. Eight months'
seniority was a matter of enormous importance. It
would affect all his subsequent career.

'Tell Mr. Bolton you have my permission to leave
the ship tomorrow, and you may use one of the ship's
boats.'

'Thank you, sir.'

'Good luck, Hornblower.'

During the next twenty-four hours Hornblower had
not merely to try to read all through Norie's *Epitome
of Navigation* again, and Clarke's *Complete Handbook
of Seamanship*, but he had to see that his number one
uniform was spick and span. It cost him his spirit
ration to prevail on the warrant cook to allow the
gunroom attendant to heat a flatiron in the galley and
iron out his neck handkerchief. Bracegirdle lent him
a clean shirt, but there was a feverish moment when
it was discovered that the gunroom's supply of shoe
blacking had dried to a chip. Two midshipmen had
to work it soft with lard, and the resultant compound,
when applied to Hornblower's buckled shoes, was
stubbornly resistant to taking a polish; only much
labour with the gunroom's moulting shoebrush and
then with a soft cloth brought those shoes up to a
condition of brightness worthy of an examination for
lieutenant. And as for the cocked hat—the life of a
cocked hat in the midshipmen's berth is hard, and

some of the dents could not be entirely eliminated.

'Take it off as soon as you can and keep it under your arm,' advised Bracegirdle. 'Maybe they won't see you come up the ship's side.'

Everybody turned out to see Hornblower leave the ship, with his sword and his white breeches and his buckled shoes, his bundle of journals under his arm and his certificates of sobriety and good conduct in his pocket. The winter afternoon was already far advanced as he was rowed over to the *Santa Barbara* and went up the ship's side to report himself to the officer of the watch.

The *Santa Barbara* was a prison hulk, one of the prizes captured in Rodney's action off Cadiz[3] in 1780 and kept rotting at her moorings, mastless, ever since, a storeship in time of peace and a prison in time of war. Redcoated soldiers, muskets loaded and bayonets fixed, guarded the gangways; on forecastle and quarterdeck were carronades,[4] trained inboard and depressed to sweep the waist, wherein a few prisoners took the air, ragged and unhappy. As Hornblower came up the side he caught a whiff of the stench within, where two thousand prisoners were confined. Hornblower reported himself to the officer of the watch as come on board, and for what purpose.

'Whoever would have guessed it?' said the officer of the watch—an elderly lieutenant with white hair hanging down to his shoulders—running his eye over Hornblower's immaculate uniform and the portfolio under his arm. 'Fifteen of your kind have already come on board, and—Holy Gemini, see there!'

Quite a flotilla of small craft was closing in on the

Santa Barbara. Each boat held at least one cocked-hatted and white-breeched midshipman, and some held four or five.

'Every courtesy young gentleman in the Mediterranean Fleet is ambitious for an epaulet[5],' said the lieutenant. 'Just wait until the examining board sees how many there are of you! I wouldn't be in your shoes, young shaver, for something. Go aft, there, and wait in the portside cabin.'

It was already uncomfortably full; when Hornblower entered, fifteen pairs of eyes measured him up. There were officers of all ages from eighteen to forty, all in their number ones,[6] all nervous—one or two of them had Norie's *Epitome* open on their laps and were anxiously reading passages about which they were doubtful. One little group was passing a bottle from hand to hand, presumably in an effort to keep up their courage. But no sooner had Hornblower entered than a stream of new-comers followed him. The cabin began to fill, and soon it was tightly packed. Half the forty men present found seats on the deck, and the others were forced to stand.

'Forty years back,' said a loud voice somewhere, 'my granddad marched with Clive to revenge the Black Hole of Calcutta.[7] If he could but have witnessed the fate of his posterity!'

'Have a drink,' said another voice, 'and to hell with care.'

'Forty of us,' commented a tall, thin, clerkly officer, counting heads. 'How many of us will they pass, do you think? Five?'

'To hell with care,' repeated the bibulous voice in

the corner, and lifted itself in song. 'Be gone, dull care; I prithee begone from me——'

'Cheese it, you fool!' rasped another voice. 'Hark to that!'

The air was filled with the long-drawn twittering of the pipes of the bosun's mates, and someone on deck was shouting an order.

'A captain coming on board,' remarked someone.

An officer had his eye at the crack of the door. 'It's Dreadnought Foster,' he reported.

'He's a tail twister if ever there was one,' said a fat young officer, seated comfortably with his back to the bulkhead.

Again the pipes twittered.

'Harvey, of the dockyard,' reported the lookout.

The third captain followed immediately. 'It's Black Charlie Hammond,' said the lookout. 'Looking as if he'd lost a guinea and found sixpence.'

'Black Charlie?' exclaimed someone scrambling to his feet in haste and pushing to the door. 'Let's see! So it is! Then here is one young gentleman who will not stay for an answer. I know too well what that answer would be. ''Six months more at sea, sir, and damn your eyes for your impertinence in presenting yourself for examination in your present state of ignorance.'' Black Charlie won't ever forget that I lost his pet poodle overside from the cutter in Port-o'-Spain when he was first of the *Pegasus*. Good-bye, gentlemen. Give my regards to the examining board.

With that he was gone, and they saw him explaining himself to the officer of the watch and hailing a shore boat to take him back to his ship. 'One fewer of us, at least,' said the clerkly officer. 'What is it, my man?'

'The board's compliments, sir,' said the marine messenger, 'an' will the first young gentlemen please to come along?'

There was a momentary hesitation; no one was anxious to be the first victim.

'The one nearest the door,' said an elderly master's mate. 'Will you volunteer, sir?'

'I'll be the Daniel,'[8] said the erstwhile lookout desperately. 'Remember me in your prayers.'

He pulled his coat smooth, twitched at his neck-cloth and was gone, the remainder waiting in gloomy silence, relieved only by the glug-glug of the bottle as the bibulous midshipman took another swig. A full ten minutes passed before the candidate for promotion returned, making a brave effort to smile.

'Six months more at sea?' asked someone.

'No,' was the unexpected answer. 'Three! . . . I was told to send the next man. It had better be you.'

'But what did they ask you?'

'They began by asking me to define a rhumb line[9] . . . But don't keep them waiting, I advise you.' Some thirty officers had their textbooks open on the instant to reread about rhumb lines.

'You were there ten minutes,' said the clerkly officer, looking at his watch. 'Forty of us, ten minutes each—why, it'll be midnight before they reach the last of us. They'll never do it.'

'They'll be hungry,' said someone.

'Hungry for our blood,' said another.

'Perhaps they'll try us in batches,' suggested a third, 'like the French tribunals.'[10]

Listening to them, Hornblower was reminded of French aristocrats jesting at the foot of the scaffold. Candidates departed and candidates returned, some gloomy, some smiling. The cabin was already far less crowded; Hornblower was able to secure sufficient deck space to seat himself; he stretched out his legs with a nonchalant sigh of relief, and he no sooner emitted the sigh than he realized that it was a stage effect which he had put on for his own benefit. He was as nervous as he could be. The winter night was falling, and some good Samaritan on board sent in a couple of purser's dips to give a feeble illumination to the darkening cabin.

'They are passing one in three,' said the clerkly officer, making ready for his turn. 'May I be the third.'

Hornblower got to his feet again when he left; it would be his turn next. He stepped out under the halfdeck into the dark night and breathed the chill fresh air. A gentle breeze was blowing from the southward, cooled, presumably, by the snow-clad Atlas Mountains of Africa across the strait. There was neither moon nor stars. Here came the clerkly officer back again.

'Hurry,' he said. 'They're impatient.'

Hornblower made his way past the sentry to the after-cabin; it was brightly lit, so that he blinked as he entered and stumbled over some obstruction. And it was only then that he remembered that he had not straightened his neckcloth and seen to it that his sword hung correctly at his side. He went on blinking

7   (H 206)

in his nervousness at the three grim faces across the table.

'Well, sir?' said a stern voice. 'Report yourself. We have no time to waste.'

'H-Hornblower, sir.   H-Horatio H-Hornblower. M-Midshipman—I mean Acting-Lieutenant, H.M.S. *Indefatigable.*'

'Your certificates, please,' said the right-hand face.

Hornblower handed them over, and as he waited for them to be examined, the left-hand face suddenly spoke. 'You are close-hauled on the port tack, Mr. Hornblower, beating up channel with a nor'-easterly wind blowing hard, with Dover bearing north two miles. Is that clear?'

'Yes, sir.'

'Now the wind veers four points and takes you flat aback. What do you do, sir? What do you do?'

Hornblower's mind, if it was thinking about any-thing at all at that moment, was thinking about rhumb lines; this question took him as much aback as the situation it envisaged. His mouth opened and shut, but there was no word he could say.

'By now you're dismasted,' said the middle face— a swarthy face; Hornblower was making the deduction that it must belong to Black Charlie Hammond. He could think about that even if he could not force his mind to think at all about his examination.

'Dismasted,' said the left-hand face, with a smile like Nero enjoying a Christian's death agony. 'With Dover cliffs under your lee. You are in serious trouble, Mr.—ah—Hornblower.'

Serious indeed. Hornblower's mouth opened and

shut again. His dulled mind heard, without paying special attention to it, the thud of a cannon shot somewhere not too far off. The board passed no remark on it either, but a moment later there came a series of further cannon shots which brought the three captains to their feet. Unceremoniously they rushed out of the cabin, sweeping out of the way the sentry at the door. Hornblower followed them; they arrived in the waist just in time to see a rocket soar up into the night sky and burst in a shower of red stars. It was the general alarm; over the water of the anchorage they could hear the drums rolling as all the ships present beat to quarters. On the portside gangway the remainder of the candidates were clustered, speaking excitedly.

'See there!' said a voice.

Across half a mile of dark water a yellow light grew until the ship there was wrapped in flame. She had every sail set and was heading straight into the crowded anchorage.

'Fire ships!'

'Officer of the watch! Call my gig!' bellowed Foster.

A line of fire ships was running before the wind, straight at the crowd of anchored ships. The *Santa Barbara* was full of the wildest bustle as the seamen and marines came pouring on deck, and as captains and candidates shouted for boats to take them back to their ships. A line of orange flame lit up the water, followed at once by the roar of a broadside; some ship was firing her guns in the endeavour to sink a fire ship. Let one of those blazing hulls make contact

with one of the anchored ships, even for a few seconds,
and the fire would be transmitted to the dry, painted
timber, to the tarred cordage, to the inflammable
sails, so that nothing would put it out. To men in
highly combustible ships filled with explosives fire
was the deadliest and most dreaded peril of the sea.

'You, shore boat, there!' bellowed Hammond
suddenly.

'You, shore boat! Come alongside! Come alongside, blast you!'

His eye had been quick to sight the pair-oar
rowing by.

'Come alongside or I'll fire into you!' supplemented
Foster. 'Sentry, there, make ready to give them a shot!'

At the threat the wherry turned and glided towards
the mizzen chains.

'Here you are, gentlemen,' said Hammond.

The three captains rushed to the mizzen chains and
flung themselves down into the boat. Hornblower
was at their heels. He knew there was small enough
chance of a junior officer getting a boat to take him
back to his ship, to which it was his bounden duty to
go as soon as possible. After the captains had reached
their destinations he could use this boat to reach the
Indefatigable. He threw himself off into the sternsheets as she pushed off, knocking the breath out of
Captain Harvey, his sword scabbard clattering on the
gunwale. But the three captains accepted his un-
invited presence there without comment.

'Pull for the *Dreadnought*,' said Foster.

'Dammit, I'm the senior!' said Hammond. 'Pull
for *Calypso*.'

'*Calypso* it is,' said Harvey. He had his hand on the tiller, heading the boat across the dark water.

'Pull! Oh, pull!' said Foster, in agony. There can be no mental torture like that of a captain whose ship is in peril and he not on board.

'There's one of them,' said Harvey.

Just ahead, a small brig was bearing down on them under topsails; they could see the glow of the fire, and as they watched the fire suddenly burst into roaring fury, wrapping the whole vessel in flames in a moment, like a set piece in a fireworks display. Flames spouted out of the holes in her sides and roared up through her hatchways. The very water around her glowed vivid red. They saw her halt in her career and begin to swing slowly around.

'She's across *Santa Barbara's* cable,' said Foster.

'She's nearly clear,' added Hammond. 'God help 'em on board there. She'll be alongside her in a minute.'

Hornblower thought of two thousand Spanish and French prisoners battened down below decks in the hulk.

'With a man at her wheel she could be steered clear,' said Foster. 'We ought to do it!'

Then things happened rapidly. Harvey put the tiller over. 'Pull away!' he roared at the boatmen.

The latter displayed an easily understood reluctance to row up to that fiery hull.

'Pull!' said Harvey.

He whipped out his sword from its scabbard, and the blade reflected the red fire as he thrust it menacingly at the stroke oar's throat. With a kind of sob, stroke tugged at his oar and the boat leaped forward.

'Lay us under her counter,'[11] said Foster. 'I'll jump for it.'

At last Hornblower found his tongue. 'Let me go, sir. I'll handle her.'

'Come with me, if you like,' replied Foster. 'It may need two of us.'

His nickname of Dreadnought Foster may have had its origin in the name of his ship, but it was appropriate enough in all circumstances. Harvey swung the boat under the fire ship's stern; she was before the wind again now, and just gathering way, just heading down upon the *Santa Barbara*.

For a moment Hornblower was the nearest man in the boat to the brig and there was no time to be lost. He stood up on the thwart and jumped; his hands gripped something, and with a kick and a struggle he dragged his ungainly body up on to the deck. With the brig before the wind, the flames were blown forward; right aft here it was merely frightfully hot, but Hornblower's ears were filled with the roar of the flames and the crackling and banging of the burning wood. He stepped forward to the wheel and seized the spokes; the wheel was lashed with a loop of line, and as he cast this off and took hold of the wheel again he could feel the rudder below him bite into the water. He flung his weight on the spoke and spun the wheel over. The brig was about to collide with the *Santa Barbara*, starboard bow to starboard bow, and the flames lit an anxious gesticulating crowd on the *Santa Barbara's* forecastle.

'Hard over!' roared Foster's voice in Hornblower's ear.

'Hard over it is!' said Hornblower, and the brig answered her wheel at that moment, and her bow turned away, avoiding the collision.

An immense fountain of flame poured out from the hatchway abaft the mainmast, setting mast and rigging ablaze, and at the same time a flaw of wind blew a wave of flame aft. Some instinct made Hornblower while holding the wheel with one hand snatch out his neckcloth with the other and bury his face in it. The flame whirled round him and was gone again. But the distraction had been dangerous; the brig had continued to turn under full helm, and now her stern was swinging in to bump against the *Santa Barbara's* bow. Hornblower desperately spun the wheel over the other way. The flames had driven Foster aft to the taffrail, but now he returned.

'Hard-a-lee!'

The brig was already responding. Her starboard quarter bumped the *Santa Barbara* in the waist, and bumped clear.

'Midships!' shouted Foster.

At a distance of only two or three yards the fire ship passed on down the *Santa Barbara's* side; an anxious group ran along her gangways keeping up with her as she did so. On the quarterdeck another group stood by with a spar to boom the fire ship off; Hornblower saw them out of the tail of his eye as they went by. Now they were clear.

'There's the *Dauntless* on the port bow,' said Foster. 'Keep her clear.'

'Aye aye, sir.'

The din of the fire was tremendous; it could hardly

be believed that on this little area of deck it was still possible to breathe and live. Hornblower felt the appalling heat on his hands and face. Both masts were immense pyramids of flame.

'Starboard a point,' said Foster. 'We'll lay her aground on the shoal by the Neutral Ground.'[12]

'Starboard a point,' responded Hornblower.

He was being borne along on a wave of the highest exaltation; the roar of the fire was intoxicating, and he knew not a moment's fear. Then the whole deck only a yard or two forward of the wheel opened up in flame. Fire spouted out of the gaping seams; the heat was utterly unbearable, and the fire moved rapidly aft as the seams gaped progressively backward.

Hornblower felt for the loopline to lash the wheel, but before he could do so the wheel spun idly under his hand, presumably as the tiller ropes below him were burned away, and at the same time the deck under his feet heaved and warped in the fire. He staggered back to the taffrail. Foster was there.

'Tiller ropes burned away, sir,' reported Hornblower.

Flames roared up beside them. His coat sleeve was smouldering.

'Jump!' said Foster.

Hornblower felt Foster shoving him—everything was insane. He heaved himself over, gasped with fright as he hung in the air, and then felt the breath knocked out of his body as he hit the water. The water closed over him, and he knew panic as he struggled back to the surface. It was cold—the Mediterranean in December is cold. For the moment the air in his clothes supported him, despite the weight of the sword at his side, but he could see nothing in the darkness, with his eyes still dazzled by the roaring flames. Somebody splashed beside him.

'They were following us in the boat to take us off,' said Foster's voice. 'Can you swim?'

'Yes, sir. Not very well.'

'That might describe me,' said Foster; and then he lifted his voice to hail, 'Ahoy! Hammond! Harvey! Ahoy!'

He tried to raise himself as well as his voice, fell back with a splash, and splashed and splashed again, the water flowing into his mouth cutting short something he tried to say. Hornblower, beating the water with increasing feebleness, could still spare a thought —such were the vagaries of his wayward mind—for the interesting fact that even captains of much seniority were only mortal men after all. He tried to unbuckle his sword belt, failed and sank deep with the effort, only just succeeding in struggling back to the surface. He gasped for breath, but in another attempt he managed to draw his sword half out of its scabbard, and as he struggled it slid out the rest of the way by its own weight; yet he was not conscious of any noticeable relief.

It was then that he heard the splashing and grinding of oars and loud voices: he saw the dark shape of the approaching boat, and he uttered a spluttering cry. In a second or two the boat was up to them, and he was clutching the gunwale in panic.

They were lifting Foster in over the stern, and Hornblower knew he must keep still and make no effort to climb in, but it called for all his resolution to make himself hang quietly on to the side of the boat and wait his turn. He was interested in this overmastering fear, while he despised himself for it. It called for a conscious and serious effort of will-power to make his hands alternately release their deathlike grip on the gunwale, so that the men in the boat could pass him round to the stern. Then they dragged him in and he fell face downward in the bottom of the boat, on the verge of fainting. Then somebody spoke in the boat, and Hornblower felt a cold shiver pass over his skin, and his feeble muscles tensed themselves, for the words spoken were Spanish—at any rate an unknown tongue, and Spanish presumably.

Somebody else answered in the same language. Hornblower tried to struggle up, and a restraining hand was laid on his shoulder. He rolled over, and with his eyes now accustomed to the darkness, he could see the three swarthy faces with the long black moustaches. These men were not Gibraltarians. On the instant he could guess who they were—the crew of one of the fire ships who had steered their craft in past the Mole, set fire to it, and made their escape in the boat. Foster was sitting doubled up, in the bottom of the boat, and now he lifted his face from his knees and stared round him.

'Who are these fellows?' he asked feebly—his struggle in the water had left him as weak as Horn-blower.

'Spanish fire ship's crew, I fancy, sir,' said Horn-blower. 'We're prisoners.'

'Are we indeed!'

The knowledge galvanized him into activity just as it had Hornblower. He tried to get to his feet, and the Spaniard at the tiller thrust him down with a hand on his shoulder. Foster tried to put his hand away, and raised his voice in a feeble cry, but the man at the tiller was standing no nonsense. He brought out, in a lightning gesture, a knife from his belt. The light from the fire ship, burning itself harmlessly out on the shoal in the distance, ran redly along the blade, and Foster ceased to struggle. Men might call him Dreadnought Foster, but he could recognize the need for discretion.

'How are we heading?' he asked Hornblower, sufficiently quietly not to irritate their captors.

'North, sir. Maybe they're going to land on the Neutral Ground and make for the Line.'

'That's their best chance,' agreed Foster.

He turned his neck uncomfortably to look back up the harbour.

'Two other ships burning themselves out up there,' he said. 'There were three fire ships came in, I fancy.'

'I saw three, sir.'

'Then there's no damage done. But a bold endeavour. Whoever would have credited the Dons with making such an attempt?'

'They have learned about fire ships from us, perhaps, sir,' suggested Hornblower.

'We may have "nursed the pinion that impelled the steel"[13] you think?'

'It is possible, sir.'

Foster was a cool enough customer, quoting poetry

and discussing the naval situation while being carried off into captivity by a Spaniard who guarded him with a drawn knife. Cool might be a too accurate adjective; Hornblower was shivering in his wet clothes as the chill night air blew over him, and he felt weak and feeble after all the excitement and exertions of the day.

'Boat ahoy!' came a hail across the water; there was a dark nucleus in the night over there. The Spaniard in the sternsheets instantly dragged the tiller over, heading the boat directly away from it, while the two at the oars redoubled their exertions.

'Guard boat——' said Foster, but cut his explanation short at a further threat from the knife.

Of course there would be a boat rowing guard at this northern end of the anchorage; they might have thought of it.

'Boat ahoy!' came the hail again. 'Lay on your oars or I'll fire into you!'

The Spaniard made no reply, and a second later came the flash and report of a musket shot. They heard nothing of the bullet, but the shot would put the fleet—towards which they were heading again—on the alert. But the Spaniards were going to play the game out to the end. They rowed doggedly on.

'Boat ahoy!'

This was another hail, from a boat right ahead of them. The Spaniards at the oars ceased their efforts in dismay, but a roar from the steersman set them instantly to work again. Hornblower could see the new boat almost directly ahead of them, and heard another hail from it as it rested on its oars. The

Spaniard at the tiller shouted an order, and the stroke oar backed water and the boat turned sharply; another order, and both rowers tugged ahead again and the boat surged forward to ram. Should they succeed in overturning the intercepting boat they might make their escape even now, while the pursuing boat stopped to pick up their friends.

Everything happened at once, with everyone shouting at the full pitch of his lungs, seemingly. There was the crash of the collision, both boats heeling wildly as the bow of the Spanish boat rode up over the British boat but failed to overturn it. Some-one fired a pistol, and the next moment the pursuing guard boat came dashing alongside, its crew leaping madly aboard them. Somebody flung himself on top of Hornblower, crushing the breath out of him and threatening to keep it out permanently with a hand on his throat. Hornblower heard Foster bellowing in protest, and a moment later his assailant released him so that he could hear the midshipman of the guard boat apologizing for this rough treatment of a post captain of the Royal Navy. Someone unmasked the guard boat's lantern, and by its light Foster revealed himself, bedraggled and battered. The light shone on their sullen prisoners.

'Boats ahoy!' came another hail, and yet another boat emerged from the darkness and pulled towards them.

'Cap'n Hammond, I believe!' hailed Foster, with an ominous rasp in his voice.

'Thank God!' they heard Hammond say, and the boat pulled into the faint circle of light.

'But no thanks to you,' said Foster bitterly.

'After your fire ship cleared the *Santa Barbara* a puff of wind took you on faster than we could keep up with you,' explained Harvey.

'We followed as fast as we could get these rock scorpions to row,' added Hammond.

'And yet it called for Spaniards to save us from drowning,' sneered Foster. The memory of his struggle in the water rankled, apparently. 'I thought I could rely on two brother captains.'

'What are you implying, sir?' snapped Hammond.

'I make no implications, but others may read implications into a simple statement of fact.'

'I consider that an offensive remark, sir,' said Harvey, 'addressed to me equally with Captain Hammond.'

'I congratulate you on your perspicacity, sir,' replied Foster.

'I understand,' said Harvey. 'This is not a discussion we can pursue with these men present. I shall send a friend to wait on you.'

'He will be welcome.'

'Then I wish you a very good night, sir.'

'And I, too, sir,' said Hammond. 'Give way there.'

The boat pulled out of the circle of light, leaving an audience open-mouthed at this strange freak of human behaviour, that a man saved first from death and then from captivity should wantonly thrust himself into peril again. Foster looked after the boat for some seconds before speaking; perhaps he was already regretting his rather hysterical outburst.

'I shall have much to do before morning,' he said, more to himself than to anyone near him, and then addressed himself to the midshipman of the guard boat. 'You, sir, will take charge of these prisoners and convey me to my ship.'

'Aye aye, sir.'

'Is there anyone here who can speak their lingo? I would have it explained to them that I shall send them back to Cartagena under cartel, free without exchange. They saved our lives, and that is the least we can do in return.' The final explanatory sentence was addressed to Hornblower.

'I think that is just, sir.'

'And you, my fire-breathing friend. May I offer you my thanks? You did well. Should I live beyond tomorrow, I shall see that authority is informed of your actions.'

'Thank you, sir.' A question trembled on Hornblower's lips. It called for a little resolution to thrust it out, 'And my examination, sir? My certificate?'

Foster shook his head. 'That particular examining board will never reassemble, I fancy. You must wait your opportunity to go before another one.'

'Aye, aye, sir,' said Hornblower, with despondency apparent in his tone.

'Now lookee here, Mr. Hornblower,' said Foster, turning upon him. 'To the best of my recollection, you were flat aback, about to lose your spars and with Dover cliffs under your lee. In one more minute you would have been failed—it was the warning gun that saved you. Is not that so?'

'I suppose it is, sir.'

'Then be thankful for small mercies. And even more thankful for big ones.'

Notes

1. *Captain Pellew*: Edward Pellew (1757-1833) entered
   the Navy in 1770 and drew attention to himself by his
   high spirits. When the Duke of York once paid a
   ceremonial visit to a ship he saw young Pellew
   standing on his head on a yardarm. Pellew saw active
   service in the War of American Independence and
   throughout the Napoleonic Wars (1793-1815), com-
   manding the *Indefatigable* 1795-99.
2. *Gig*: The captain's personal boat.
3. *Rodney's action off Cadiz*. Rodney (1719-92) defeated
   the Spaniards off Cadiz in 1780 and so raised the siege
   of Gibraltar.
4. *Carronades*: ships' guns with large calibre but with
   short barrels, firing a large quantity of small shot.
5. *Epaulet*: the ornamental shoulder-piece worn on
   uniform by higher ranks but not by a midshipman.
6. *Number ones*: best uniforms.
7. *Black Hole of Calcutta*: J. Z. Holwell was commandant
   of a fort at Calcutta which the Nawab of Bengal
   stormed in 1756. Holwell afterwards claimed that 146
   persons were imprisoned in an almost airless cell, with
   the result that all but 23 died.
8. *Daniel*: Daniel was put into a lion's den.
9. *Rhumb line*: The curve described upon the terrestrial
   spheroid by a ship sailing on one course.
10. *French tribunals*: courts that tried aristocrats during
    the Reign of Terror (1793-4).
11. *Counter*: the curved part of a ship's stern.
12. *Neutral Ground*: the strip of land between Gibraltar
    and Spain.

13. '*Nursed the pinion that impelled the steel*' : Foster is quoting Byron, *English Bards and Scotch Reviewers*:

> 'So the struck eagle, stretched upon the plain,
> No more through rolling clouds to soar again,
> Viewed his own feather on the fatal dart,
> And winged the shaft that quivered in his heart;
> Keen were his pangs, but keener far to feel
> He nursed the pinion which impelled the steel.'

In the same way the British are now suffering from a weapon, the fire-ship, that they have initiated. (To be exact, Foster could not have quoted this line, because it had not yet been written!)

SATURDAY AFTERNOON

Stella Gibbons (Mrs. A. B. Webb) was born in London in 1902. Her father was a doctor in a poor district of North London and her childhood was clouded by the surroundings. She was the eldest of three children and before she could read she used to entertain her brothers with telling stories of her own invention. She was educated at North London Collegiate School and London University. She has always been deeply interested in the lives of ordinary people, such as we meet in 'Saturday Afternoon'. Her best-known book is Cold Comfort Farm, *a burlesque of country-life novels. She has also published several volumes of short stories and her* Collected Poems *were published in 1950.*

She lives in Highgate. Her recreations are gardening and reading.

●

One o'clock on Saturday afternoon.

Suddenly the sirens began. Their sound swooped into the basement kitchen at 46 Marling Street, Camden Town, and put Mrs. Spenk in mind of an air-raid, as they did every Saturday. She was scuttling around the kitchen laying the stained cloth with three places when the noise began, and when she heard the first uncouth howl from Sheer's Tobacco Works just

round the corner she glanced despairingly at the
clock and darted across to the stove, and thrust a
knife down into the potatoes.

They were not done. Nor was the cabbage. Nor
was the stew. And in ten minutes Spenk would be
home from Sheer's wanting his dinner, and young
Cissie too. Oh, what was the matter with Saturday,
that everything went wrong and made you want to
scream the place down? It was the same every
Saturday (slap! went the vinegar down on the table
beside the crusted egg-cup that held the mustard)
—try as she might, nothing would go right of a
Saturday.

'All be'ind, like the cow's tail, I am this morning,'
muttered Mrs. Spenk, rummaging in the bread crock
under the mangle. She looked like a cross goblin in
the dim kitchen, with her hair lifted off her worried
little face and her hollow temples, and coiled on the
top of her head in the style of thirty years ago.

'Eat—eat—eat—like a lot of 'orses. Cloth never
gets off the table, Saturdays.'

She shoved a vase of marigolds, withering in stale
water, into the middle of the table. Even the flowers
looked dull in the kitchen, where the only vivid thing
was the beautiful red and gold fire, roaring proudly
behind its bars like a lusty lion. The shiny brown walls,
brown oilcloth, and grey ceiling were nets for darkness, and outside there was no sunlight.

To and fro scurried Mrs. Spenk, pitching wet
potato peelings into the dustbin, opening a tin of
peaches. In the midst of her dartings (and the cabbage stems still hard as wood!) slow steps began

descending the area steps, and glancing angrily out
between the lace curtains she saw the large silhouette
that was more completely familiar to her than any
other in her narrow world.

He came into the kitchen, and his experienced eye
took in the bare table, the agitated saucepans, and
his wife's angry face. His own, tired and dirty and
already sullen, became lowering.

'Ain't it ready yet, then?'

'No, it isn't. I'm all be'ind this morning. You
know I 'ad to take Georgie down to the Ear 'ospital and
they kep' me there the best part of an hour. You're
early, aren't you? 'Tisn't more than ten pars'.'

'I'm orlright. You 'urry up them saucepans.'

He pushed past her across the room, and went into
the little scullery, where she heard him having a bit of
a wash while she slopped some stew on to a half-warm
plate.

The sound of his leisurely preparations made her
furious.

She called sharply:

'Where are you off to, s'afternoon?'

'Down to the Bridge with Charlie Ford.'   His
sullen voice beat back her shrill irritation with a flat
wall of secrecy. She muttered something about a
waste of money, but he pretended not to hear.

He came back into the room with his face washed
clean and looking startlingly different. He was fifty,
and flabbily stout, but his unfulfilled youth seemed
petrified in the immature curves of the lips behind
his moustache and in the uncertain expression of his
eyes.

He glanced furtively across at his wife as he sat
down to his plate of stew, but said no more. He kept
looking up at the alarm clock on the mantelpiece
between his half-masticated mouthfuls, for the match
began at 3.15, and it took a good hour to get down
to Stamford Bridge. At twenty to two he got up,
putting on his bowler. Mrs. Spenk, who had started
on her own stew, neither looked up nor spoke. The
air of the kitchen was charged with waves of resent-
ment that rolled from the taut, raging little woman
to the big sullen man.

The monotonous hours of the week, spent by him
in a vast air-cooled impersonal room shaken by
machines, and by her in a little underground room
smelling of stale food, had fused once again into the
mutual nervous hatred of Saturday afternoon. Every
week it was the same. Neither knew what was the
matter. They only felt angry and tired out. By
Saturday afternoon Mr. and Mrs. Spenk were no
longer a man and a woman. They were the results
of a fact called the social system.

Another piece of the system came slowly down the
steps as Mr. Spenk was going up; his daughter Cissie,
aged sixteen, who earned thirty shillings a week as a
junior-typist-cum-switchboard-operator in a paper-
pattern shop in the Strand. Usually Cissie was cheer-
ful, but now Saturday afternoon had got her too.
She was coiled in on herself in a satisfying fit of
temper about nothing.

'Ullo, Dad.'

'Ullo. You been sacked yet?' he asked, dis-
agreeably.

This was a sore point, for Cissie was impertinent, and seldom kept a job longer than three months. But she was too depressed to flare back at him. She turned her face away, muttering, 'Oh, shut up, do,' and slouched past him down the steps and in at the dark door.

Outside the light was so lowering that dusk seemed only just round the corner. The pavements were greasy. The sticks of celery in the baskets at street corners shone white as bones. Mr. Spenk bought a paper, and settled down to half an hour's strap-hanging in a carriage full of men in spotty suits and cloth caps. Charlie Ford had failed to turn up; and he was alone. He felt no better. His pipe tasted sour, and there was nothing much in the paper. A fool trod on his corn in the scramble at Charing Cross. He hated everybody.

His face was set in sullen lines as he climbed the grass-grown steps to the shilling tiers. He felt that if he didn't get a good position against the barriers he would kick up a shine, demand his money back, raise blasted hell. But he got a good place all right, plumb opposite the grand-stand. A huge, massed semicircle of pink dots curved away from him on either side, topped by thousands of cloth caps of pinkish-grey, greeny-brown, speckled grey. The air was warm and heavy, and did not carry the flat roar of thirty-five thousand voices.

After an unseeing stare round, Mr. Spenk settled down to his paper, and to wait.

Cissie went straight over to the glass by the window

and began squeezing earnestly at an invisible spot on her white chin, staring into her face with passionate interest as though she had not seen it for six months.

She was still staring, and pawing the spot discontentedly with one finger, when her mother came in, dressed to go out. Cissie did not turn round.

'Well, my lady! What's the matter with you? Got out of bed the wrong side this morning, like your father? Don't you want no dinner?'

'Don't fancy stew. 'S always stew, Saturdays. I'm not 'ungry.'

'Go without, then. Only don't go pickin' about in the safe after I'm gone out. I want this 'ere for supper.'

Cold stew and vegetables were being slammed into the safe.

'Where's Georgie?' asked Cissie, who wanted to be sure the house would be empty that afternoon.

'Upstairs with Mrs. P. 'E don't want no dinner, neither. 'Is ear's too bad, 'e says.'

Coals were shot noisily into the range and damped down with the colander of tea-leaves from the sink, while Cissie stood in maddening idleness with all this energy whirling round her, trying how her hair looked with a centre parting.

Not until she heard the door slam, and her mother running angrily up the area steps, did she turn round. Then she turned suddenly, staring at the kitchen already settling into winter twilight, with the red eye of the fire now burning sulkily. Cissie gave a loud and animal yawn, stretched, stared again, and suddenly tore across the kitchen and upstairs into the

bathroom which the Spenks shared with the rest of
the house.

She began to let hot water furiously into the bath,
twizzling the taps round and round, using up the
Saturday night bath water.   Her round face was
youthful and tired as a cross fairy's under its paint.
Every few minutes she yawned extravagantly, and
the steam, which was already warming the tiny, dank
cell deliciously, was drawn down into her lungs.

She locked the door. She lit the gas. She crumbled
a twopenny packet of bath salts into the discoloured
bath, and began to undress.

Mrs. Spenk, fussing up the steps of the house next
door, found young Mrs. Judd waiting; dark, severe,
and like a gipsy.

'There you are,' she exclaimed, 'I was just wondering if I wouldn't come along and fetch you.   But
there, I said to myself, I expect she's been kept. I
know what Saturday is.'

They ran down the steps rapidly together, as though
no precious second must be wasted.

'There's a 47,' said Mrs. Spenk, as they crossed
the road. 'We'd better take it. The big picture starts
at a quarter to three, and if there's anything I do
hate it's coming in in the middle of the big picture.'

The Majestic Cinema was already lit up when they
arrived; and the lights were on inside the hall,
diffusing that languid, warmly coloured glow which
prepares the mind of the audience to receive dreams.
Outside, the greasy streets were lost in cold shadows.
Inside, the tall gold curtains streamed to meet the

benign glow and the walls were stippled with a gold
on whose bland expanse shone ruby and amber lights.

Mrs. Spenk and Mrs. Judd were shown into two
good seats in the middle of the hall, and they sat
down. Mrs. Spenk, with lips pressed bitterly together, sat upright in her ruby-covered seat. Nevertheless, its curves caressed her taut spine. Neither
woman spoke as they sat waiting for the lights to
fade; and the eyes of both were turned upwards to
the rich, mysterious folds of the curtain hiding the
screen.

Mr. Spenk, waiting under a lead-coloured sky
with fifty-thousand other spectators (for the ground
had filled rapidly) still felt no better. He huddled
himself up with his pipe and stared sourly in front
of him. The idle roar from the crowd poured up to
the dim clouds; it was waiting, no more; relaxed as
an enormous animal.

Suddenly, at ten past three, there was a satisfied
stirring and a murmuring. The teams were running
down the sloping alley-way underneath the grandstand, pretty as a ballet in their blue and red and
white shirts, and white shorts. They scattered across
the grass, livid green in the lowering light, and began
to punt the ball about. The satisfying dull 'ponk!'
as they kicked it whetted the crowd's appetite; it was
in the very mood that once presaged gladiatorial
combats.

The visiting team won the toss. Mr. Spenk stolidly
watched the preliminary punting, saw even the kick-
off without settling down comfortably to a critical

absorption in the game, as he usually did at once. Play began badly. It was not good football. Lowther, the squat, dark Scotsman in whom the crowd was most interested, scurried down the field like a crab, hugging the ball when he should have passed and passing when he should have shot.

Backwards and forwards swayed the crowd, following the ball. Now the bright figures clotted in front of one goal, now in front of the other; now they spread out along the grass; but still the play did not improve. The crowd began to feel famished, like an animal with forbidden food dangled before its eyes. It wanted the food of swift, accurate, triumphant action expressed through the bodies of the players. It could feed on such action, and release through it the energy imprisoned in its own myriad devitalized bodies. Still such action did not come.

But suddenly the game improved. The crowd began to rock faster. Loud, short roars broke its watching silence. The crowd-animal was at last eating its food of swift, fierce action. Excitement began to pump into the dead air above the stadium.

'Oh, angel boy! Oh, pretty!' cried a lyric voice above the long roar as Charlton, the visiting goalkeeper, leapt four feet in the air, striking the ball yards out of the net.

Mr. Spenk was really watching now. He was eating his food with the rest of the crowd. Presently he, like the rest of the crowd, would begin to feel better.

The lights were fading. A long beam shot across

the darkness and ghostly words shone suddenly
behind the curtains, which parted with a rippling
noise. Dreams were about to be made.

Neither Mrs. Spenk nor Mrs. Judd saw the notice
of the censor's approval, the names of the author,
director, and photographers, or the names of the
cast. For them the big picture did not begin until
a lovely giantess appeared on the screen, petulantly
asleep in a billowing bed. Gerda Harbor in 'Gay
Lady'.

Their eyes followed her awakening as solemnly as
the eyes of children, while their ears accepted without
offence the disdainful nasal cadences of her voice.
The luxury of her bedroom, which their eye had
scarcely time to absorb, pointed no contrast between
itself and the rooms in which they slept. They were
like two children listening to a story.

Mrs. Judd, better informed, nudged Mrs. Spenk
when the hero appeared.

'That's Orme Roland. 'E always acts with Gerda
Harbor. Isn't 'e a lovely feller?'

'Nice-lookin', but a bit thin on top, ain't 'e?'
objected Mrs. Spenk. In spite of the dream-weaving
silver beam and the shadows that were created to
absorb into themselves all the tiredness and vague
discontent in the audience, the taint of Saturday
morning still soured Mrs. Spenk's tongue. But her
pose was less rigid in her seat. No one else was
sitting upright. The audience was chiefly young men
and women; and each girl rested her head on the
thin shoulder of her boy. Darkness, lies and dreams
fed these children of the machine age like the pictures

in the crystal of a Persian magician. The machines
wove dreams; their children watched; and forgot
their slavery to the weavers.

' 'E's been married three times,' observed Mrs.
Judd.

' 'As 'e now? Fancy! It's a wonder anyone in
'Ollywood would 'ave 'im, after that. Still, I suppose
it don't mean the same to Americans as it does to us.
'E is a nice-lookin' feller, and no mistake. She's
lovely, too. I like that way of doin' 'er hair.'

Mrs. Spenk, also, was beginning to feel better.

Just before half-time, United equalized. Now at
twenty past four, the Pensioners wanted a goal to
win. They attacked like vigorous yet cold-thinking
demons. Each rush was planned. Lowther, at last,
was awake. His crab-like scurries, in which the ball
seemed tied by an invisible wire to his toes or his
heel, brought roars of ecstasy from the crowd. Mr.
Spenk roared with the rest. He stood on tiptoe to
roar and see the better. When Fordy, the visiting
team's inside-right, steadied himself—shot—shot too
high and struck the bar, Mr. Spenk joined in the
terrible impatient groan that went up.

' 'Ow's Lowther doin' now?' asked a voice, trium-
phantly.

' 'E ain't doing so badly,' admitted another voice.
'Seems a bit too fond of the ball, though. Might
'ave treacle all over it, the way it sticks to 'im.'

'Half an hour ago you said 'e was afraid of it.
Cor! there ain't no pleasin' some people.'

'Orlright, don't upset yourself. Fact is, you take

football too seriously. It ain't like 'orse-racin'.'

The moonlight rippled on the lake in the million-aire's garden. There was a party, and the house was lit up, and distant music in the ballroom floated from the windows. But outside on the terrace they were alone—those two—the mocking beauty in black velvet and the tall man in faultless evening-dress. His hand slipped over hers—he bent towards her . . . but she slipped from him, lightly as her own scarf that waved in the moonlit air.

'Shall we dance?'

'I never cared for dancing—until now.'

Arm in arm, they passed into the great house, the woman smiling dazzlingly into the man's eager eyes.

'Leadin' 'im up the garden,' murmured Mrs. Spenk, and Mrs. Judd, watching raptly, nodded.

At last! Over his head and slam into the net! The visiting goalkeeper sprawled on his face; and then, across the dusky field, skirred the whistle for 'time'. The crowd rocked and roared for nearly a minute while the teams were going off the field, but already people were working their way towards the exits.

Mr. Spenk, having re-lit his cold pipe (it tasted good again), ambled up the tiers and joined the slowly swaying herds of people on their way to the gate. He stopped for a moment or two at the stone barrier along the top tier and stood looking down on the crowd; a large, amiable chap at whom no one would look twice. He had seen some good football. That was worth seeing, that was.

He sleepily adjusted his bowler and pipe, and stumped down the steps. The satisfied crowd-animal, swaying home under the darkening sky into the lit streets, ate him up.

They began the kiss.

Slowly, very slowly, so that the audience might savour in its full strength this moment for which it had been unconsciously longing, his hands fell upon her shoulders. She stared up into his suffering face, with a tender smile at the corners of her lips. Tears brightened her great eyes, and her hair was adorably disordered. She had been crying. He had been mad with rage. Now he was angry no longer. The strain between them had relaxed, deliciously, and the audience relaxed as well. He drew her close to him. Her head went tilting back, with its fleece of fairest angel hair. His arms drew her closer, closer. Slowly, in deliberate ecstasy, their lips touched at last. The curtains swung together to a burst of music as the two figures faded out.

'Lovely!' sighed Mrs. Spenk, groping for her hat. 'I *did* enjoy that. 'Aven't enjoyed anything so much for months.'

Back through the streets where the mud now shone in the lamp-light like a paste churned from jewels came Mr. and Mrs. Spenk by their separate ways, both soothed, rather sleepy, and amiable.

But as Mrs. Spenk and Mrs. Judd turned out of the jolly rattle of Camden Town High Street into Marling Street, where it was darker and quieter,

Mrs. Spenk's spirits fell.   She remembered that Cissie was sulky, and Tom had the rats, and there was tea to get.   There was no end to it.   Whenever you had a bit of fun, you had to pay for it.   Oh, well, it was all in the day's work.

She said good night to Mrs. Judd at the top of the area steps and ran down.   A light shone in the kitchen, and the blind had been pulled down over the lace curtains.

Cissie was standing exactly where she had stood three hours ago, in the same position; in front of the glass, with her face screwed sideways the better to pick at the invisible spot on her chin.

' 'Ave you been there all the afternoon?' asked her mother, good-naturedly, hanging up her coat and hat behind the door.   'You won't 'ave no face left if you pull it about much longer; you'll wear it away.'

Cissie did not turn round.   But her thin back, whose shoulder-blades showed under a clean pink blouse, looked friendly.   She said, mildly:

'The kettle's boiling.   I got tea for you.'

'That's a good girl.   Dad 'ome?   Where's Georgie?'

'Still upstairs with Mrs. P.   He says his ear's better. Dad won't be home for another half an hour, I shouldn't think.   The paper says there was nearly fifty thousand down at the Bridge this afternoon.'

Mrs. Spenk was putting four heaped spoonfuls of tea into the brown pot, and glancing critically over the table to see if Cissie had forgotten anything. The table looked nice.   Cissie had put on a clean cloth and fresh water in the marigolds.   There was a new pot of jam and half a pound of yellow cake.

The gaslight softened the rusty colours in the kitchen into warmth, and the kettle was singing. The fire was gold.

Mrs. Spenk poured the water on the tea, murmuring: 'We won't wait for Dad,' and sat down opposite Cissie, kicking off her shoes. She stared across at her daughter.

'Well—you *are* all dressed up like a dog's dinner. Where are you off to, tonight?'

'Nowhere, reely,' putting up a small red hand, with pointed shiny nails, to her hair. 'I may be goin' out with Millie Thomson a bit later.'

'Your eyebrows, Cissie Spenk! 'Oo are you supposed to look like—Anna May Wong or what?'

'Oh, I wish they'd grow quicker, so's I could pluck 'em more often,' said Cissie, earnestly. 'I love pluckin' 'em. I like to make 'em so thin you can't hardly see I've got any at all.'

Mrs. Spenk's caustic rattle of laughter was interrupted by Mr. Spenk.

'Ready for tea, Dad?'

'I could do with a cup. You never saw such a sight as there was down at the Bridge; must have been over sixty thousand down there. Took me the bes' part of an hour, getting away.'

Mrs. Spenk and Cissie looked interested, but each woman wondered how men could so waste their time and money.

Tea was then eaten, in a warm, comfortable silence. It was half-past six. The nervous misery of Saturday morning had gone over into the repose of Saturday night. In front of the Spenk family lay a fair prospect

twenty-four hours long, called 'termorrer's-Sunday';
a day on which no one need get up early, and huge
meals were eaten all day.

After tea Cissie went off mysteriously to meet
Millie Thomson. Mrs Spenk piled the dishes up in
the scullery with one eye on the clock, for her
shopping was not yet done. The second kettle had
boiled while they finished tea, and she now splashed
the water over the dirty dishes.

Mr. Spenk had drawn his chair to the fire, with
a paper and his pipe. But there was an uneasy thought
at the back of his mind which interrupted his comfort.
He tried to ignore it, but it came back. It was the
memory of Saturday morning, blent with another
emotion too vague to name.

At last he got up heavily, and went out into the
scullery. He held out his hand to his wife for the
drying-cloth. She, flushed and busy in the candle-
light and the steam, stared at him blankly.

'Give you a 'and,' said Mr. Spenk.

'Well, I never! Miracles will never cease!' cried
Mrs. Spenk ironically.

But she smiled at him as she flipped across the
drying-cloth.

DESMOND HAWKINS

A MAN AND A FOX

*Desmond Hawkins wrote this story when he lived in Essex,
combining the writing of fiction with the breeding of ducks
and geese. Later he joined the B.B.C. as a producer and is
now Head of West Regional Programmes.*

His publications include Sedgemoor and Avalon, *a
description of a part of Somerset; a study of Thomas Hardy
in the* English Novelists *Series; and an anthology in the*
Everyman Library *of the writings of D. H. Lawrence.*

'A Man and a Fox' first appeared in Penguin New
Writing.

•

Like most writers, I take books too seriously. The
book I was reading warned me against over-indulging
geese. They are hardy birds, accustomed to live day
and night in the open, and it is misplaced zeal to shut
them in a house or shed at night. I could see the point
of this, but I was uneasy. I was thinking of the fox.
No doubt there is more than one fox in these parts,
but we always speak in a quintessential way of 'the
fox': much as we speak of the devil, disregarding the
diversity of evil spirits. There had been rumours
about the fox. May lost a pullet, Jack's wife had lost
some chicks. What was worse, the hunt no longer paid
compensation. Worst of all, the hunt did not even

intend to remove the plaything which it cherished so dearly in time of peace.[1]

It was at this point that I took the book too seriously. I read that 'it is an uncommon fox that will brave the wrath of a gander'. I looked at my ganders that evening with new eyes. I admired their formidable air. And when the sun went down I left them cruising about in their methodically painstaking way, pecking tirelessly at the meadow.

I was still uneasy when I awoke next morning. I ran to the window and began to count. The sun was up, the white plumage of the birds glistened like sails against the meadow green. The number was right, they were all there. It was not until I looked again that I began to wonder why one—or was it two?—was so disinclined to move with the others. I must have stood staring out of the window wondering uneasily for some moments. I had the authority of the book to reassure me. I was surprised by the lack of faith which sent me racing down the stairs and up into the meadow. How was I to know that the book had omitted the pertinent fact that the fox-dispelling wrath of a young gander is greatly inferior to the invincible fury of a gander of riper years?

I picked up the first carcase. A few feathers drifted away through my fingers in a fine haze of whiteness. Head and neck were gone. The body was ripped from keel to crop. A second one lay twenty yards off. The fox had stepped out of the book, an actual invader pacing the meadow at dawn.

I imagine he came up from the water-meadow, keeping close to the hedge as it curves. In the thin

fume of mist, as the sun came up above the further
hill, the cows would look indifferently at the creeping
intruder crouched under the burden of his perpetual
guilt, convicted and damned by his every furtive
movement.   At the boundary of my field he could
push through a rabbit-run in the hedge bottom, or
work his way along the dry ditch.   And then the
insidious snake-like weaving through the tall grass,
the silent ambush.

The goose was still warm in my hand.   I know
nothing that shows more beautifully proportioned
curves from every angle than a goose.   It has the
entire complacent roundness of prosperity, it is the
figure of God's bounty.   I looked at the gashed
symmetry of whiteness, the sagging intestines. Flecks
of blood on the gleaming snow of the breast were in
their way as startling a sabotage as a bomb thrown in
the village post office.

I went round to see Jack. 'Fox has been to mine
now,' I said.

'Has?' he answered, opening his eyes wide in a sort
of half-comically exaggerated alarm which would have
been just right for, say, news of tigers in the district.
'Get anything?'

'Two of my geese,' I said, with very great feeling.
On occasions such as this I notice that men always
overdo it a bit. We stood in stern silence. Somehow
the whole security of the village seemed to be at stake.
My blood was up.

'Look, Jack,' I said, 'have you got a gun I can
borrow?'

Jack opened his old eyes again and grinned.   He

could not have shown a more illicit and accessory delight if I had proposed to batter sharp-tongued Mrs. Pridey to death.

'You can have it,' he said. 'You know how to handle it, do you?'

Next morning I was away at daybreak with Jack's gun under my arm. I find that a gun acts like a trans-forming wand on a man's character. One becomes the hunter with a mere touch of the barrel. As I crossed the home meadow I felt particularly self-contained, in a kind of autonomous and splendid isolation—as if in the last resort I could pull the triggers and blast my way through a hostile world. Or perhaps it is that the hunter in his concentration takes on some of the identity of his quarry. The craft of hunting is obvi-ously homoeopathic.

Under the damson tree there is an old iron bed-stead-top which May stuck into the hedge to stop her cows from breaking through. I climbed on to the bed, grabbed the tree and swung down into the ditch on the other side. For many mornings that was to be my routine. The old bed and the damson tree seemed to mark the frontier between my own everyday world and that other foreign world which the fox inhabited (though in an understandably elusive fashion). As I stood in the ditch, on the outward journey, I cocked my triggers; when I came to the bedstead, on my return, I removed the cartridges. It was the dividing line.

I confess I was a little disillusioned when I came back the first morning without having so much as seen the fox. In my heart I had felt it was principally a matter of getting up early enough. A few more blank mornings modified my ambition—I would be content to start humbly with a distant view of the beast. Assassination would follow as I advanced in familiarity. I began to collect reports which gave me a guide to his habitual route. I plotted a course for him from the wood above the sandpit, along the hedge which lies like a girdle about the waist of what we call 'the hills' (these in terms of the Essex landscape being a gentle undulation gathered up beyond the village), and so to the water-meadow. From this strategic point he could strike impartially at three or four of us. The spot is marked by a rough gate, and whoever holds the gate dominates the view to the four corners of the compass. Clearly the wise tactician would get there before first light and hide.

This plan became an obsession with me. I had taken a great pride in my geese, and I was determined to avenge them. Their killing had been so wanton an affront as to be intolerable. I admit this must sound grotesque to anyone who has never raised geese, but there it is—I was smarting under an injustice and I was going to wipe it out. And so, each time I finished my share of patrolling the village at night (for these were the days of the blitz), I picked up Jack's twelve-bore and made off 'into the hills'.

Patience did have its reward in the end, though not in the way I had expected. I used to stand rigidly still, moving my head very slowly, fancying that in the end the fox would move into view, slinking along by one hedge or another, coming nearer and nearer. But it was not like that at all. I had been watching a hare, I remember, across the stream, as it first pottered about and then streaked off in a long, wild dash. And suddenly, in the foreground, there was the fox—or rather, the vixen. She stood about ten or a dozen paces clear of the hedge, on the hither bank of the stream. A moment before she had been invisible: now she stood, vivid and gleaming in the early sunshine, with her curious hangdog indolence—the head cowering, the mouth apart with that remorseless caricature of a grin that makes one think of crocodiles.

I had, of course, rehearsed this moment a thousand times in my imagination. She was standing still, looking about her, ignorant of my presence. The wind was in my favour. There was only the mere formality of pulling the trigger, and then I could walk back to the village, carrying her in a nonchalant way. I think I have never coveted anything so much in all my life.

As I took aim I had some misgivings about the range. Ten paces nearer would make absolutely certain. But the vixen was standing on the edge of a patch of wheat: one move from me and she would be into it. I held my breath and squeezed the trigger. I was trembling with excitement. It seemed too good to be true, for I have not lost my town-bred wonderment that I can stand and stare at a vixen within sight of my house. And in the stillness of daybreak, before the first tractor starts to drone and men's voices begin to come across the fields, that abrupt silent apparition out of nowhere was almost like an illusion.

Her haunches bucked violently as the shots hit her. She lurched over sideways and then dived into the wheat. And that was my last view of her that morning.

My near-miss gave me a measure of success in the village. I was at pains to tell the story in a very dramatic way, and I suppose no one had thought I could even wound a fox. Moreover, as I began to stress the great distance between the vixen and myself —and it did indeed seem to increase each time I thought of it—it was quite a matter for wonder that I had hit the thing at all. There were neighbourly comments on the notorious difficulty of killing a fox outright except at absolutely point-blank range.

Nevertheless, I was not satisfied. I had had it almost in my hands, and it had slipped through. It seemed impossible that one could come within inches of success and return empty-handed. In the daytime I inspected the wire netting round my pens, in the evening I fastened my birds in securely, and all the time I felt mocked by the fox. More and more I wanted to get away across the fields, and hide, and wait, and watch. It was a duel that had to be fought out to some sort of conclusion. My original confidence was gone, but I kept on in a dull stubborn obstinacy. It somehow upset the conventions of my world to be menaced by something that I could not master. I had grown up to believe that plain burglary was dealt with by the police so thoroughly that there is no need for the private citizen to turn vigilante. However, life in the country has a way of upsetting all such notions of delegation to specialists: the sensible man takes the precaution of being 'handy' in as many trades as possible. It is a lesson learnt from hard experience, that the plumber, the midwife, the fire brigade, the vet and the rest of them so often arrive too late.

Yet I had to thank the fox for one good thing. It got me out of bed early, and it gave me a routine. Now I have always supported the view that middle-aged gentlemen ought to be able to take a walk, if a walk is what they want, without pursuing the vagaries of a golf ball. But I must admit that, by the same argument, I ought to be able to stroll across the meadows to the 'hills' without carrying a gun and looking for a fox. Why had I never done it? I suppose pure contemplation is a too intangible aim for most of us. We stumble into it by accident, as an aside of a practical occasion. To 'see the country' is somehow an unsatisfactory goal. Logically it should be right to have no other preoccupation, to concentrate wholly on the aesthetic of Nature—but is not the keenest observation always quickened by some limited and practical purpose? 'Beauty' is a very diffuse focus of detail, compared with the precise attention of the poacher, the shepherd, the angler and the orni-thologist. I never learnt any landscape so well as the beat from the bedstead under the damson tree to the gate by the 'hills'. I know the particular tussock that looks so remarkably like a rabbit, the place in the ivy-twined elm where the wood pigeon comes clapping out as I pass, the gap in the clay bank where the barbed-wire is easiest to crawl through. As I turn the angle of the hedge into the last meadow there is the familiar line of pollard willows by the stream. I have climbed up their broad platforms where thin blades of grass grow, and mosses, and small seeds lie scattered. In the hedge beyond, the usual pair of magpies are chattering their machine-gun conversation.

This is one piece of England that I know, probably better than anyone alive. It is something precious to me, for no other reason than that I know it so intimately and fully. In broad daytime it is commonplace enough: I think of it as it is when the sky begins to show the first streaks of light and the grass is heavy with dew, when the rabbits are about and the Little Owl has not finished the night's hunting. And for that discovery I have to thank the fox.

One morning I shot a rabbit. I was pleased with the result, which demonstrated to any fox in the vicinity that I was still about and could shoot straight enough —but I had to admit an infidelity to my main purpose. In the first fury of my fox-hunting I had pledged myself to let nothing distract me from my chosen target. Shooting rabbits betrayed my presence and unmasked my intention. I was for the fox or nothing at first.

But as the weeks passed I lost the fine edge of my fanatical zeal. Harvest was all but in; the partridges were cruising contentedly across the stubbles; and in those first autumn days the tension of the countryside slackens. The very land seems to go easy. Sugar beet and potato remain, but they are only pendants to the central drama—a sort of silver age after the golden glory. When the north-easter begins to freshen a little across the stubble one realizes that the fortunes of the year are mainly settled. I began to entertain the thought that the fox had defeated me.

After I had shot the rabbit I became less careful about creeping up to the top gate and hiding there.

I caught the holiday mood of the harvest fields and went rambling along the hills, without bothering to keep myself out of view—like a sightseer on yesterday's battlefield. I carried the gun, of course, but I was not expecting to use it. It had simply become a habit, a part of my walking costume.

The first stretch of the hills was standing with potatoes, the vines a deep, almost bottle-green, but more lush—a great square of bold, rich colour that is not praised enough. Beyond the potatoes there had been wheat, but now it was all carted. I stood with my back to the hedge and looked up the empty stubble as my eye was caught by something moving. The sun was coming up over the shoulder of the hills, shining into my eyes. I peered again, distinguishing three or four animals racing round in circles in the distance. They looked too big for hares, more dog-like in build. I watched them stop, and race round again, and move together in a group. The utter silence made them seem uncanny. At first I could hardly believe my eyes.

My first problem was to get within some sort of range. If I moved forward from the hedge I should be seen before I had made a dozen paces. I thought of lying down and wriggling forward on my stomach, but the distance was great and the stubble gave no cover whatsoever. I was baffled. And then I noticed a shallow ditch running alongside the potatoes, with a feathering of wild grasses on either bank to make things easier. I worked my way back, close to the hedge, and got on my knees in the ditch. It was barely two feet deep and rank with weeds that were carrying a

heavy dew. I dared not raise my head. I guessed the
distance to where the foxes were playing and started
to crawl, taking care to keep my gun-barrels from
fouling.

Twice the ditch ended and drained under a cross-
over from the potato field to the stubble. At the first
one I drew myself up, wriggled forward snake
fashion, and re-entered the ditch. At the second I
stopped and raised my head to see where I was.

The foxes were some forty or fifty paces ahead—
a dog fox, a vixen and four cubs, with the sun behind
them. They had not detected me, for they were all
playing carelessly, chasing one another and rolling
over in a sort of mock battle. The silent ease of movement, the weaving patterns of the running forms and
their profound absorption were like some fantastic
ballet. It was an unforgettable sight, with the sun
now clear of the line of the hills, and the cubs
tumbling delightedly on the stubble.

I raised my gun slowly and sighted the dog fox.
He was hardly in range, but I enjoyed looking along
the barrels and seeing him on my sight. For some
time I just lay in the ditch, watching him like that—
with a sort of joy that I had at last hunted him down.
And this time I was in no hurry. I watched him with
that peculiar lethal tenderness which the winner
instinctively feels for the loser.

What was the victory? I think it was that I had got
to the innocent heart of the fox's world, and I could
understand Blake's argument[2] that the Devourer has
his proper place in the Creation—'for the Prolific
would cease to be Prolific unless the Devourer

received the excess of his delights.' There is a frontier between the cultivated and the raw: and when we see the frontier we must admit that Man is never entirely the master of his world. If all our works were to vanish there is an alternative order that would swarm back across the undefended frontier; and the constant threat of that eternal counter-attack is personified—for the English imagination—in the fox, the last of the predatory wild beasts, the toy souvenir of grimmer days. This seems to me the true ritual of the fox-hunt: a symbolical conquest of Nature, made in the humility of our knowledge that the conquest is never final nor complete. The fox retains a reversionary interest in Man's estate.

Something of this I began to understand as I eyed the fox along the length of my gun, although my mind was making no such phrases. Rather was I wondering if his lordship would oblige me by stepping a dozen paces nearer. I was reluctant to miss him. He stood sniffing the fresh morning air and looked indifferently across the potatoes. Then he advanced slightly towards me and stopped again, idly, without alarm. It was a toss-up whether he walked right into my gun, or dived into the potatoes. I decided to let him make his own choice—I was not going to fire unless he came within dead-certain range. It is difficult not to sympathize with one's enemy, if you brood over him long enough. Prosperous men, I notice, have strange impulses of picaresque ambition; and how many of us are so cosy within the law and the conventions that we never in fancy play at running with the fox? Indeed, nothing we create quite escapes the moment of disgust when we turn to devour—and re-create.

And so, to my great surprise, I was almost relieved when the fox—from being entirely motionless— suddenly plunged into the potatoes and vanished. The decisive quickness of movement was astounding. I looked again to be sure he was not still standing, or slinking towards me. Nothing. The great field was still and empty. Vixen and cubs, supposedly playing on my right, had also gone. It was as if I had never seen them.

I came home whistling contentedly. At the bed-stead I stopped and lit my pipe. The geese were clamouring to be let loose in the meadow. I had a line of Thoreau's[3] running in my mind, and I kept trying to recall the exact words: 'We hunt in order that we may learn to love—and when we love, we no longer want to hunt.' Is that it?

Notes

1. *In time of peace*: The story was written in war-time.
2. *Blake's argument*: William Blake (1757-1827) says this in *The Marriage of Heaven and Hell*. A main theme of this book is that contraries are essential to existence— 'Thus one portion of being is the Prolific, the other the Devouring'. So destructive animals like the fox have their essential place in Creation.
3. *Thoreau*: Henry David Thoreau (1817-62), the famous American nature-lover, gave up business to live a simple and solitary life in the woods. He wrote *Walden or Life in the Woods*.

E. L. MALPASS

RETURN OF THE MOON MAN

E. L. Malpass was born at Derby in 1910. He was educated at King Henry VIII School, Coventry, and afterwards went to work in a bank. During the Second World War he served in the R.A.F., and it was only after the War that he began writing. He has had a number of stories published and broadcast, and his first novel, Beefy Jones, *has recently been published.*

At Christmas, 1954, The Observer *organized a competition for short stories set in the year A.D. 2500, and 'Return of the Moon Man' won the first prize. A collection of the prize-winning stories was published under the title* A.D. 2500.

Generally speaking a story must convince us, while we are reading it, that it is true. This story is a specimen of comic fantasy, and few readers are likely to believe it: indeed its best effects come from placing the most improbable events in a humdrum setting.

●

A.D. 2500. That was the year they brought the Electric to Pen-y-Craig Farm.

Wonderful it was, when Grandfather Griffiths

pressed down the switch, and the great farm kitchen
was flooded with light. There was Dai my Father,
and Mother, blinking and grinning in the light, and
Electric Plumber Williams, smug as you please,
looking as though he had invented the Electric himself
and sent it through the pipes. Only Gran was sad.
Tears streaming down her face, she picked up the old
paraffin lamp and carried it sadly out into the scullery.

That was funny about Gran. She was progressive,
and left to herself she would have filled the house with
refrigerators and atomic cookers and washers. But
Grandfather called these things devil's inventions, and
would have none of them. And yet, when Grandfather at last agreed to the Electric, Gran was in tears.
Reaction, Auntie Space-Ship-Repairs Jones said it was.

'Well,' roared Grandfather. 'There's your Electric.
But don't think because you've talked me into this
you'll talk me into any more of these devil's inventions. Let no one mention the words space ship in my
presence ever again.'

That was intended for Gran. In her black clothes she
was a rather pathetic looking little woman, and no
match at all for her fiery husband. But one thing she had
always insisted that she wanted; a space ship; and it
had been a source of argument between them for years.

I tell you all this that you may know that we of
Pen-y-Craig are not the backward savages that some
people would have you believe. We are in touch with
modern thought, even though we are apt to cling to
the old ways. But what I really remember of those
far-off, golden days of 2500 is of how the first Expe-
dition to the Moon set off, and of how it landed in

Ten Acre Field, and of the strange events that followed.

Men had been trying to set off for the Moon for years, perhaps for centuries. But you know how it is. Something always happened to stop them. The weather was bad, or someone's aunt died, or there was an eclipse. In the autumn of 2500, however, they were ready at last.

It was cold that evening, and we were sitting by the fire, enjoying the Electric. Grandfather was listening in; suddenly he jumps to his feet and shouts, 'Blasphemy'.

No one took much notice, for if the old man didn't jump up and shout 'Blasphemy' at least once of an evening Gran thought he was sickening and gave him a purge.

So Gran said dutifully, 'What is it, Mortimer?'

'Flying to the Moon, they are,' he cried. 'The space ship has just left London. And they're dancing in the streets, and exploding fireworks in celebration. Sodom and . . .'

But at that moment there was a noise as of a great wind passing over, and then a terrible crash as though someone had picked up all our milk churns and dropped them on the Dutch barn. We ran outside and there, in Ten Acre Field, a Thing was glinting in the frosty moonlight. Huge it was, like a great shining rocket.

Grandfather looked at it. 'Lost their way, maybe,' he said with malicious satisfaction. Then he felt in his waistcoat pocket and took out a card and put it in my hand.

10

'Run you, Bronwen,' he said, 'and give them the business card of Uncle Space-Ship-Repairs Jones.'

But I was frightened, being but a little girl, then, and clung to my mother's skirts. So Dai my father started up the tractor without a word, and rode off to fetch Uncle Space-Ship-Repairs Jones.

Down to the farm came the Moon Men, as the newspapers called them, their helmets bright in the moonlight, and soon Dai my father arrived. My Uncle was sitting on the tractor with him, clutching a great spanner and grinning as pleased as Punch, and soon his banging and hammering came across the still air from Ten Acre.

One of the Moon Men took off his great helmet.

'Bit my tongue when we landed sudden,' he said.

'Nothing to what you will bite when you land on the Moon,' said my Grandfather.

'That is what I am thinking,' the man replied. 'And that is why I say they can have their old Moon. Back to Golders Green by first train it is for me.'

The Leader took off his helmet at that. 'Go to the Moon one short?' he cried. 'That would never do.

'I will go in his place,' said Dai, my Father, quietly.

'You go? Never,' roared my Grandfather. 'No son of mine shall go gallivanting round the planets.'

My Father flushed angrily. But no one argued with Grandfather and at that moment we heard Uncle Space-Ship-Repairs Jones holloaing that the Moon-Ship was now right as ninepence.

The Moon Men, all except one who had bitten his tongue, set off for Ten Acre.

'I will come and see you off,' said Grandfather,

and we watched him walk up the hill with the men.

With a great roar the Moon-Ship rose into the sky, and climbed among the stars. Soon we could see it no more.

'Supper now,' said Gran.

We got the meal ready, and then someone said, 'Where is Grandfather?'

All the grown-ups looked uneasy, and suddenly I was frightened and began to cry.

'Gone to talk to the old bull, maybe,' said Gran.

Silently my Father picked up the lantern and went out into the fields. It was a long time before he came back.

'Gone,' he said. 'Clean as a whistle.'

No one said anything.

Grandfather did not come back all night.

Nor the next day.

Gran was worried.

Then, at dusk, Read-All-About-It Evans, instead of dropping out evening papers from his helicopter as he flew past, landed. He marched into the house and thrust the paper under my Father's nose, and said, 'See you.'

'Octogenarian on Moon,' said big headlines. Then, below: 'Radio flash from Moon party says Mortimer Griffiths, elderly Welsh farmer, took place of member of crew injured in earth landing.'

'Well, there is sly for you,' said my Father. 'Going out for five minutes and finishing up on the Moon.'

Gran said nothing. But she went to the pegs and got her coat and went out of the door.

'Go with her, Bronwen,' my Father ordered me, but kindly.

When I got outside it was almost dark, but a big, full Moon was just swinging clear of the hill, and I could see Gran going along the path that leads up Break Back and past Ten Acre and brings you to the Little Mountain. Though I was only a child I knew where Gran was going, and why. At the top of Little Mountain she would be nearer to the Moon than anywhere. I also felt, child though I was, that she would want to be alone, so I followed quietly, at a short distance.

Sure enough, Gran kept on up the mountain, and at last we were on the top place where there is no-thing but broken rocks, and holes of black water, and lonely old ghosts. And the Moon was well up now, and so near that you felt that if you stood on tiptoe you could touch it like an apple on the tree.

Gran looked at the Moon. And the Moon looked at Gran.

Now Grandfather was a big man, and I knew she was hoping to see him, perhaps putting up a little tent, or lighting a Primus. But there was no sign of anyone on the Moon's face. And at last, after a long time, Gran shivered and sighed. Then she muttered, 'Round at the back, maybe,' and she turned and came slowly down the mountain. And though she must have seen me she said no word.

The next night the same thing happened. At moon-rise Gran set off for the mountain, and I followed. But this time the Moon was not quite round, and

Gran looked at it for a long time. Then she said,
'Shrinking it is,' and came home again.

This happened every night. The Moon grew
thinner and thinner, and Gran went out later and
later. Young though I was, they let me stay up till all
hours to follow Gran up the mountain. But at last
the Moon rose so late that Dai my Father said, 'Bed
for you tonight, my girl.'

But I woke up in the small hours, and looked out,
and there was the Moon, a thin, silver sickle, and
there was the yellow light of a lantern climbing the
dark side of the sleeping mountain.

I put on my coat and ran out into the cold.

When I reached the top of the mountain Gran was
there. To my surprise she spoke to me. Pointing to
the thin crescent she said, 'Hanging on by his finger
nails now he will be,' and she took my hand and led
me home.

The next morning she said to my Father, 'What
time does the Moon rise tonight, Dai?'

My father looked at the paper.

'There is no Moon tonight, Gran,' he said.

'No Moon,' repeated Gran in a voice of death.
'No Moon.' She rose, and hung a black cloth over
the big picture of Grandfather at the Eisteddfod.

'Falling through the sky he will be now,' she said
slowly, as though speaking to herself. 'Like a
shooting star he will fall, and like a shooting star he
will cease to be.' She went back to her chair and sat
down, her hands folded in her lap.

'But the fact that you can't see the Moon doesn't
mean it isn't there,' my Father explained. 'It's just

that the sun is shining on the other side of it.'

Gran gave him a look. 'Black midnight,' she cried. 'Black midnight, and you talk to me of sunshine. Open the door.' She pointed an ancient finger at it. 'And, if the sun is shining, run up Snowdon barefoot I will, like the mad woman of Aberdaron.'

Dai my Father gave up. There was a silence. Then Gran began talking again, almost to herself.

'He was a hard man,' she said. 'I didn't much care for him. Never would he buy me anything. A space ship, only a little one, I asked him for, many times.

' "No mention of space ships in the Lives of the Great Saints", he says, smiling nasty, putting the tips of his fingers together, smug as you please.

' "No mention of indoor sanitation either," I say, real angry now. "But that do not stop Rev. Williams having a little room up at the Manse."

'But it was no good. There was no arguing with Mortimer Griffiths.' She rose, and went to bed. And next day she left for Aberystwyth and married Llewellyn Time Machine.

They went to 1954 for their honeymoon. And two days after they had gone Grandfather came back from the Moon.

'Finished the Harvest?' he asked.

'Yes,' said my Father.

'Have you mended the fence in Ten Acre?'

'Never mind the fence in Ten Acre,' said my Father. 'Gran has married Llewellyn Time Machine.'

That was a terrible moment. For a long time my Grandfather stood stroking his beard. Then suddenly he shot out his long arm and grasped a chopper.

'Where are they?' he roared. 'Where are they?'

My father, pale, said nothing.

Grandfather seized him by the throat and shook him.

'Where are they?' he repeated.

'In—in 1954,' gasped my Father.

Grandfather let him go.

'Get the tractor out,' he ordered.

'Where are you going?'

'1954,' said Grandfather.

He was gone for nearly a week.

Then he came back, alone. He was in a good mood, quite talkative, for him.

'Hired a Time Machine in Llandudno,' he said, beaming. 'Chased them right back to the Middle Ages. Llewellyn caught the Black Death. And I smashed his Time Machine to pieces with my little chopper.'

'And Gran?' asked my Father.

'Stranded in the Middle Ages, with no money, and no means of getting back,' said Grandfather with immense satisfaction. 'She was taking the veil when I last saw her. Damp, the nunnery looked. Damp and cold.

'Teach her to go hankering after space ships,' said my Grandfather.

AUDRIE MANLEY-TUCKER

WANTED—A MIRACLE

Audrie Manley-Tucker has served in the W.R.A.C., been a commercial traveller, worked in a Probation Office and run her own typing bureau. She first tried her hand at writing seven years ago and has since had hundreds of magazine stories and serials published. She says that at school she was hopeless at most things except English, and like the girl in the story she could not sing a note. She is fond of travel and of being near the sea and she is also interested in antique shops, people and books.

●

The first snowflakes were hurrying to meet her as Dilys came from school; but she felt no joy in their feathery kisses, neither did she visualize a cloak of white laid across the valley, where the curled petals drifted. The remembered humiliation of the afternoon still scorched her too fiercely.

She walked slowly through the playground and down the street to the hump-backed bridge. There she stood, staring down into the sullen press of black water—a dark, secretive child, black hair flowing smooth and straight to her shoulders.

Again, she lived an afternoon's agony and shame that had begun when Miss Roberts lifted her baton and rapped on the music stand for silence. . . .

Miss Roberts was new to Bryngwyn School, and she had promised that she would lift them to the heights of achievement. They should bring back the Cup from the Three Valleys' Musical Festival, did they but practise enough. The talent was there, she said; this very afternoon, they would sing to her, class by class, and she would know who was good enough to be chosen for the School Choir.

Dilys had sung desperately, fear like a tight knot inside her, but those finely attuned ears of Miss Roberts missed nothing; three lines, and then she rapped furiously on the music stand. Her voice had a deadly quietness, as penetrating as the raw cold outside.

'Some one,' she said softly, 'is not singing in tune. We will begin again.'

The whole class knew who it was and felt the disgrace sharply. Their eyes sidled towards Dilys and away again, and the warm pink tide raced into her cheeks. She stood, taut as a bowstring, her fists bunched tightly in the folds of her tunic.

Please God, she prayed, let me be able to sing, just this once! Miss Brown never cared much for singing; when the notes came wrong and the class all laughed at me, she said that not every one could sing in tune. But she was English; and you know, God, it is a terrible thing not to be able to sing, if you are Welsh.

But the prayer was lost somewhere among the grey fleece of cloud that made a carpet for His Feet; and the verse must be sung again, at once. Desperately, she willed the notes to come right. They spilled out flat and toneless, pebbles flung into a sweetly running stream of sound.

Thirty pairs of eyes rested accusingly on Dilys; a small flicker of scornful laughter ran through the class, like wind rippling the corn.

Thirty-one pairs of eyes. . . . Miss Roberts' were bright and hard and angry.

'You, Dilys Morgan! Singing out of tune for fun, are you? Do you not want to be chosen for the Choir?"

'No!' Desperation made the monosyllable sound defiant and sullen.

'Oh!' Thick, black brows shot up half an inch. 'You do not want to sing, and so you will not. But indeed you will—every verse of the carol, out here by my desk. And we shall listen!'

Dilys stood there, terrified, immovable, the palms of her hands wet and slippery.

'Come now, Dilys!' The voice had an ominous calm-before-the-storm quality.

Dilys shivered. 'I—can't—sing!' she pleaded.

'That I do not believe. Quickly, I am waiting!'

She came slowly to the desk, on lead-weighted feet. Thirty pairs of eyes watched, fascinated, the tightly folded mouth. Dilys closed her eyes. Perhaps by this time, her prayer had reached God, and he would send music out from her lips, clear and sweet and true. She backed her petition to Him with every promise she could think of: no more playing truant from Sunday School, no grumbling when Mam wanted her to run an errand, all her pocket money should go to the Missions. . . .

But God was deaf, when she sang:

> In the bleak mid-winter
> Frosty winds made moan,
> Earth stood hard as iron,
> Water like a stone;
> Snow had fallen, snow on snow . . .

Her tuneless words were lost beneath the laughter. Bitter hatred of Miss Roberts flared within her, a passionate storm of anger for the wound exposed. 'I won't sing any more, ever!' she cried.

Miss Roberts' mouth was hard; twin spots of colour burned in her sallow cheeks. The calculated insolence of the child! Very well, then!

The others went home early, and Dilys stayed half an hour late, laboriously copying a passage from *David Copperfield* in her neat handwriting; and to the burning humiliation was added a sense of injustice, and sudden rage against God. . . .

Leaning over the bridge, Dilys thought how angry she was with Him. That was a dreadful thing, surely, to be angry with God? But then He must have been very angry with her when she was born, to have given her a voice with no music in it.

She stared at the heavy sky above terraces of houses huddled along the shoulder of mountain, above the inquisitive fingers of tall, brick chimneys, and the ugly sprawl of the pithead. The snow was coming down faster, sugar frosting on a cake, glittering under street lamps that were beginning to bloom like yellow chrysanthemums.

And she only wanted to die; to be free for ever from

the memory of this afternoon, lost in the black torrent of the river beneath her. . . .

The Reverend Ivor Jones passed her on his way home to tea; paused suddenly, struck by the dejection in the thin, hunched shoulders, and crossed to her side. 'Dilys Morgan! Time you were going home for your tea, surely?'

'I don't want any tea.'

Mr. Jones looked down at his Sunday School pupil with a sense of shock; so much bitterness for such a young face! 'Something wrong, is there?' he asked.

The tight little knot of misery within her would not dissolve into words. She shook her head, two tears squeezing out from under closed lids.

Mr. Jones, with four nice, uncomplicated children of his own, had an unfailing remedy for every ill of the heart: give the hands something to do.

'When you go home,' he said, 'ask your Mam if she will spare you this evening. Edryd Evans has finished the wooden figures for the Crib, and you shall fetch them for me. Then we will make the Manger Scene in the Chapel.'

She nodded, without speaking, and he went away feeling slightly snubbed. Dilys watched him climb the steep, cobbled hill before she turned homewards.

'Late enough you are, Dilys,' her mother scolded gently. 'School came out long ago.'

'I was down by the bridge,' she said.

'In this cold?' Still scolding softly, her mother poured the tea. By the fire her father dozed, home from the pit. Looking at him, Dilys remembered the time last year when he had sung *Myfanwy* at the Men's

Club, and her mother had cried, hearing him. And whenever she, Dilys, sang, there would be only laughter.

After tea she said: 'I saw Mr. Jones, Mam. I am to fetch the little figures for the Crib from Edryd Evans, and then help make the Manger Scene.'

She went out into the snow-filled darkness. Tomorrow, the bleak grey valley would be soft and white, all the sharp lines smudged into softness, all the ugly places rubbed out by the snowfall.

She passed two small boys, like pink-cheeked cherubim, singing carols by lantern light; in the Institute, the Choir was practising, their voices deep and rich, reminding her strangely of Granny Aberbeeg's plum-cake. And then the voices of the women soared above them, clear and as thin as flutes. All Wales sang, except Dilys Morgan, with whom God was angry.

Edryd Evans' house was the last in a row of miners' cottages, along by the railway line. His garden was a square patch of beaten black earth, overshadowed by a ramshackle workshop.

He was working by the light of two hurricane lamps, when Dilys pushed open the door—a little shrivelled apple of a man with iron-grey curls. Beside his chair were propped the crutches which had helped him to walk for forty years. On his bench, midst the delicate whorls and curls of wood chippings and the fine snow of sawdust, lay the tools of his trade; and along the window-ledges stood jars of paint like potted rainbows. In front of him lay an unpainted figure of a woman in a full-skirted dancing dress. Cupped in one hand he held a little kneeling Cherub, with baby wings and folded hands, and with a paintbrush Edryd was giving him a robe the colour of sunlight.

Dilys stood, hesitant, on the threshold, blinking in the strong white light. 'Mr. Jones asked me to come for the figures. . . .'

Edryd looked up; his eyes darkly brilliant in a wrinkled nut-brown face saw deeper than the surface of things. No child should ever look like that, he thought, laying down Cherub and paintbrush.

'For the Manger figures?' he said.

His fine, delicate hands gently lifted a strip of cloth shrouding the tiny group and there was the Bethlehem story on the work bench. Carved Madonna, bent over a tiny crib, her cloak the bright, burning blue of Southern seas. Tall Joseph, hands curved around his staff; three kneeling Shepherds on one side, their crooks touched to their foreheads, three brilliantly coloured Wise Men on the other side. And over them all brooded an Angel, so tall that his wings were curved protectively around the little scene. In his fingertips he held the shining Bethlehem Star—pure fancy, a whimsical touch that was Edryd's own.

'Isn't it lovely?' Dilys sighed, the torment within still for a moment. Tentatively she touched a gilded wing. 'Do you really make all these from wood?'

He picked up a small, rough block. 'From pieces like this. Smoothed and chiselled and carved they must be, and then painted.'

'Does it take a long time?'

He shrugged, smiling at her. 'What is time, if you are doing something that makes you happy?' He

began to wrap the figures carefully in cloth, and all
the time his bright, kind eyes watched Dilys. 'Not
happy, are you?' he said. 'Why?'

She could not tell him, at first. She just stared
down at the deft hands, and thoughts of the afternoon
ached sharply within her.

'Something hurts,' said Edryd, 'very deep within
you. Talk of the hurt and the ache is less. . . .'

Gently, with infinite patience, he coaxed the tale
from her.

'When did you know,' he said softly, 'that you
could not sing?'

She frowned. 'Always, I think. Mam would say:
"No blackbird is our Dilys, eh?" and Dad would laugh
and say not to worry. And then in school, Miss
Brown laughed, but it was a kind laugh, see?'

'And some laughter is cruel,' Edryd told her, 'and
some people with silver tongues have no understanding in their heads, like your Miss Roberts. Of
course, it is a sad thing, not to sing, and you living in
the Valleys.'

'God was angry, I think. Or else I should have
been able to.'

Edryd sighed. For these things there was no answer,
any more than there was adequate answer for the
crutches. A man just accepted; but it was a hard
thing for a child to accept, a child who cried, as Dilys
did: 'I want to sing! I want to sing, and the notes
won't come right!'

'The music is there, wanting to get out, a little
bird in a cage,' Edryd said. He searched for words of
comfort, and they came suddenly like an illumination.

'Why do you not sing, Dilys, fach? Because it is
another kind of music that is within you; to paint
beautiful pictures, or carve, or chisel things from
stone; that is singing and God, who is not angry at all,
but a very wise Person, has locked up the gift inside
you. . . .'

'But what is it? And why can I not sing as well?'

'Such greediness, indeed! He has made it so great
a gift, that there is no room for anything else. If you
could sing with your voice as well as your hands, you
would grow too proud.'

Only half understanding, she stared down at her
broad palms, her long, sturdy fingers. Singing with
the hands, was it? Making beautiful things, the way
Edryd made them.

There was a strange feeling in her fingertips. It was
almost as though she could reach out and hold things
—strange, intangible things that she only dimly
understood—as though clay and wood and stone
moulded themselves beneath her touch. Not that she
could explain these things, then. Only years after,
did she remember how she had felt, standing there
that winter evening in Edryd Evans' little workshop. . .

He watched her walk away through the yard, with
wrapped figures, all springtime in her step. He went
on painting the Cherub, with slow, rhythmic strokes
smiling to himself; and You, he said to himself as he
worked, You must make this thing right for her, You
must give her some kind of song to sing. . . .

The strange feeling stayed with Dilys all that magic
evening. It had stopped snowing as she left Edryd,
and the stars were out. One star, like a great pearl,

hung low over the Valley, high above the Chapel where Mr. Jones was waiting for her.

Seeing her tranquil face, he congratulated himself on knowing exactly how to handle children. Give them something to do, that was all; make them feel important. . . .

In the dim little grotto lit with one blue lamp, she arranged the Manger Scene. The shining star glittered in the faint lamplight, the gold-crowned Wise Men seemed almost to stir as though tired of kneeling for so long, Joseph leaned forward a little to see the Babe better. . . .

Mr. Jones, the musty-smelling little Chapel, the starlit Valley outside, dissolved and were lost to Dilys for a moment of time, as she bent close to the kneeling Madonna.

'Please,' she whispered, 'let me sing with my fingers. Tell me how I can sing with them, for my voice comes all wrong, even for Christmas carols. . . .'

Who is to say that Dilys did not see a swift, sweet smile on the carved face under the blue hood? A trick of shadows, of course, the way the light fell just at that moment—such things are always rooted in reason. . . .

The walls of the Chapel were round her again, and Mr. Jones was there, at her elbow. 'Very pretty, that, Dilys. Very pretty indeed you have made it look.'

But she was already gone, down the cobbled hill to Edryd Evans' cottage, running through the frosted, starlit night as though her feet had borrowed an angel's wings.

In a few moments, she stood, blinking, in the sharp, white light again. 'Mr. Evans, I know what I could do! Just now, I knew it, up in the Chapel! I could carve from wood the way you do, and make things. . . .'

Edryd looked at the shining face; something in it held him silent, until she asked breathlessly: 'Will you teach me, then, Mr. Evans? Will you?'

He scooped up a pile of shavings, clearing a small space on the work bench. 'Gladly,' he said quietly. 'Perhaps this is your song. My song comes to an end soon.'

She had not heard him. She was holding a rough piece of wood in her hands, holding it as carefully as though it were a fragile porcelain. . . .

It was a strange thing for a girl to want to do, the Morgans would often say, apologetically. Oh, there was rare skill in her fingers, no denying that. But—woodcarving!

In time their apologies ceased to be uttered. That was long after Edryd Evans slept in the little mountain-side cemetery and Dilys was grown into a tall young woman. Because then, tales of her skill went far beyond the Three Valleys. Angels and dancing children and Nativity scenes, and scenes from the Bible, all of them exquisitely carved in wood were to be found in the big shops. And the Welsh Ladies' Choir in their steeple-crowned hats and red shawls, each with her tiny sheet of music, no bigger than a postage stamp—and real notes of music carved on it, mind you—or playing the harp, or sitting at a tiny carved harmonium. Never one with a baton, though.

A young man came from the offices of a glossy

magazine, to take pictures of Dilys' work room.

He first shaped into words the particular magic that lay in her work.

'It seems,' he wrote, 'as though they all lingered at the brink of a song—these little Welsh Choir Ladies, that tall angel, that laughing boy . . . at any moment, they will sing, you say. The song is there, locked behind their carved lips. If sculpture is a poem in stone, then these things I have seen are songs carved in wood, and their melody is the sweeter for being unheard.'

———— ⊏O⊐ ————

THE MAN OF THE HOUSE

Frank O'Connor (born in 1903) is an Irishman whose
parents were poor and who, as an only child, was thrown
very much upon himself, so that he learned to read when
very young. Most of his education was acquired in a public
library and he later became a librarian by profession.
During the Irish Rebellion he was secretly active in the
Republican cause. He has written several plays and has
broadcast and written much about the art of the theatre.
Before the last war he was a Director of the famous Abbey
Theatre in Dublin. Among his collections of short stories
are Crab Apple Jelly, The Common Chord, Traveller's
Samples *and* Selected Stories (1956). *His stories are*
strongly Irish, dramatic, humorous, often beautiful. He is
not concerned with conventional incident, but with bringing
to vivid life the world around him. Some of his stories have
been re-written, he says, twenty, thirty, even fifty times.

●

As a kid I was as good as gold so long as I could
concentrate. Concentration, that was always my
trouble, in school and everywhere else. Once I was
interrupted I was lost.

It was like that when the mother got the bad cough. I remember it well, waking in the morning and hearing it downstairs in the kitchen, and I knew there was something wrong. I dressed and went down. She was sitting in a little wickerwork chair in front of the fire, holding her side. She had made an attempt to light the fire but it had gone against her.

'What's wrong, mum?' I asked.

'The sticks were wet and the fire started me coughing,' she said, trying to smile though I could see she was doubled up with pain.

'I'll light the fire and you go back to bed,' I said.

'Ah, how can I, child?' she said. 'Sure I have to go to my work.'

'You couldn't work like that,' I said. 'Go on up to bed and I'll bring you up your breakfast.'

It's a funny thing about women, the way they'll take orders from anything in trousers, even if 'tis only ten.

'If you could make a cup of tea for yourself, I'd be all right in an hour or so,' she said and shuffled feebly towards the stairs. I held her arm and she plonked down on the bed. I knew then she must be feeling bad. I got more sticks—she was so economical that she never used enough sticks—and soon I had the fire roaring and the kettle on. I made her toast as well; I was always a great believer in buttered toast. I thought she looked at the cup of tea rather doubtfully.

'Is that all right?' I asked.

'You wouldn't have a sup of boiling water left?' she said.

' 'Tis too strong,' I agreed with a trace of disappointment I tried to keep out of my voice. 'I'll pour half it away. I can never remember about tea.'

'I hope you won't be late for school,' she said anxiously.

'I'm not going to school,' I said. 'I'll get you your tea now and I'll do the shopping afterwards.'

I was rather proud of myself, the cool way I had said I wasn't going to school and the mother's acceptance of it. I washed up the breakfast things, then I washed myself and went up with the shopping basket, a piece of paper and a lead pencil.

'I'll do the messages now if you'll write them down,' I said. 'Would I get the doctor?'

'Indeed,' said my mother anxiously, 'you'll do nothing of the kind. He'd only want to send me to hospital. You could call at the chemist and ask him to give you a good, strong cough bottle.'

'Write it down,' I said, remembering my own weakness. 'If I haven't it written down I might forget it. And put ''strong'' in big letters. What will I get for the dinner? Eggs?'

Like the doctor, that was only a bit of swank because eggs were the only thing I could cook, but the mother told me to get sausages as well in case she got up.

It was a lovely sunny morning, and on my way to the cross I had to pass the school. There was a steep hill opposite it and I stood there for a full ten minutes staring. The schoolhouse and the sloping yard were like a picture, except for the chorus of poor victims through the opened windows, and a glimpse of Danny Delaney's bald pate as he did sentry-go near the front door with his cane behind his back. That was grand. It was nice too, chatting with the fellows in the shops and telling them about the mother's cough. I made it out a bit worse than it was, to make a good story of it, and partly in hopes that she'd be up when I got home the way we could have sausages for dinner. I hated boiled eggs.

When I got in I rushed upstairs at once and found Minnie Ryan with her. Minnie was a middle-aged woman, gossipy and pious but very knowledgeable.

'How are you feeling now, mum?' I asked.

'I'm miles better,' she said with a smile, taking the cough bottle I had got her.

'She won't be able to get up today though,' Minnie said very firmly.

'I'll put on the kettle and make a cup of tea for you so,' I said.

'Wisha, I'll do that for you, child,' said Minnie at once.

'Ah, you needn't mind, Miss Ryan,' I said. 'I can manage all right.'

'Wisha, isn't he great?' I heard her say in a low voice as I went downstairs.

'Oh, as good as gold!' exclaimed my mother.

'Why then, there aren't many like him,' said Minnie with a sigh. 'The most of the children that's going now are more like savages than Christians.'

In the afternoon my mother wanted me to play but I wouldn't go far. I remembered my own weakness. I knew if once I went a certain distance from the house I should drift towards the Glen, with the barrack drillfield perched on a chalky cliff above; the

rifle-range below it, and below that again, the mill-
pond and mill-stream running through a wooded
gorge—the Rockies, Himalayas or Highlands according to your mood. Concentration, that was what I had
to practise.

Evening fell; the street-lamps were lit and the
paper-boy went crying up the road. I bought a paper,
lit the lamp in the kitchen and the candle in the bedroom, and read to my mother from the police court
news. I wasn't very quick about it because I was only
at words of one syllable, but she didn't seem to mind
that.

Later, Minnie Ryan came again and as she was going
I went to the door with her.

'If she's not better in the morning I think I'd get the
doctor to her,' she said, not looking at me at all.

'Why?' I asked in alarm. 'Do you think is she
worse, Miss Ryan?'

'Ah, sha, no,' she said, giving her old shawl a tug,
'but I'd be frightened of the pneumonia.'

'But wouldn't he send her to hospital, Miss Ryan?'

'Ah, he might and he mightn't,' she said, leaving
me in no doubt of what he'd do. 'But that itself,
wouldn't it be better than neglecting it? If you had a
drop of whisky you could give it to her hot with a
squeeze of lemon in it.'

'I'll get it,' I said at once.

The mother didn't want the whisky, because of the
expense, but the fear of the hospital and the pneumonia was strong on me and I wouldn't be put off. I
had never been in a public-house before and the crowd
inside frightened me.

'Hullo, my old flower,' said one tall man, grinning at me diabolically. 'It must be ten years since I seen you last. One minute now—wasn't it in South Africa?'

My pal, Bob Connell, told me how he once asked a drunk man for a half-crown, and the man gave it to him. I was always trying to work up courage to try the same thing, but I didn't feel like it just then.

'It was not,' I said. 'I want half a glass of whisky for my mother.'

'Oh, the thundering ruffian!' said the man, clapping his hands. 'Pretending 'tis for his mother and he had to be carried home that night in Bloemfontein.'

'I had not,' I shouted on the verge of tears. 'And 'tis for my mother. She's sick.'

'Ah, let the child alone, Johnnie,' said the barmaid, and then I went off and got the lemon.

My mother fell asleep after drinking the hot whisky, but somehow I couldn't rest. I was wondering how the man in the pub could have thought I was in South Africa, and blaming myself a lot for not asking him for a half-crown. A half-crown would be very handy if the mother was sick. When I did fall asleep I was wakened by her coughing, and when I went in to her she was rambling in her speech. It frightened me more than anything that she didn't know me, and I lay awake in dread of what would happen if it really was pneumonia.

When she was no better in the morning the depression was terrible. After giving her her breakfast I went to Minnie Ryan.

'I'd get the doctor at once,' she said firmly.

To get the doctor I had to go first to the house of a Poor Law Guardian for a ticket to show we couldn't pay, and then to the dispensary. After that I had to rush back, get the house ready and prepare a basin of water, soap and towel for the doctor to wash his hands.

He didn't come until after dinner. He was a fat, loud-voiced man, and, like all the drunks of the medical profession, supposed to be 'the cleverest man in Cork if only he'd mind himself'. To judge from the way he looked he hadn't been minding himself much that morning.

'How are you going to get this now?' he growled, sitting on the edge of the bed with the prescription pad on his knee. 'The only place open is the North Dispensary.'

'I'll go, doctor,' I said at once.

' 'Tis a long way,' he said doubtfully. 'Do you know where it is?'

'I'll find it,' I said.

'Isn't he a great little chap?' he said to the mother.

'Oh, the best in the world, doctor,' she sighed. 'A daughter couldn't be better to me.'

'That's right,' he said. 'Look after your mother while you can; she'll be the best for you in the long run. . . . We don't mind them when we have them,' he added to my mother, 'and then we spend the rest of our lives regretting it.'

I didn't think myself he could be a very good doctor, because, after all my trouble he never washed his hands, but I was relieved that he said nothing about the hospital. I went to the door with him to see him off.

'Sure, she won't have to go to hospital, doctor?' I said.

'Not with a good nurse like you to mind her,' he said, patting my shoulder and blowing his whisky-breath in my face.

The road to the dispensary led first uphill through a thickly-populated poor locality as far as the barrack which was perched on the hill-top, and then descended between high walls till it suddenly almost disappeared in a stony pathway with red-brick corporation houses to one side, and on the other, a wide common with an astounding view of the city. The pathway dropped away to the bank of a little stream where a brewery stood, and from that, far beneath you, the opposite hillside, a murmuring honeycomb of houses whose noises came to you, dissociated and ghostlike, rose to the gently rounded top with a limestone spire and a purple sandstone tower rising out of it. It was so wide a view that it was never all lit up together; the sunlight wandered across it as across a prairie, picking out a line of roofs with a brightness like snow or delving into the depth of some dark street and outlining in shadow the figures of climbing carts and straining horses. I was full of noble ideas. I made up my mind that I'd spend the penny my mother had given me on a candle to the Blessed Virgin in the cathedral to make her better quick. I felt sure I'd get more value in a big church like that so close to heaven.

The dispensary was a sordid hallway with a bench to one side and a window like a railway ticket office at the end. There was a little girl with a green plaid

shawl about her shoulders sitting on the bench. She
gave me a quick look and I saw that her eyes were
green too. I knocked at the window and a seedy,
angry-looking man opened it. Without listening to
what I had to say he grabbed bottle and prescription
from me and banged the shutter down again without
a word. I waited a minute and then lifted my hand
to knock a second time.

'You'll have to wait, little boy,' the girl said
quickly.

'Why will I have to wait?' I asked.

'He'll have to make it up,' she explained. 'He
might be half an hour. Sit down, can't you?'

'Where are you from?' she went on after I did. 'I
live in Blarney Lane.'

I told her, and then she asked me who the bottle
was for.

'My mother,' I said.

'What's wrong with her?' asked the girl.

'She have a terrible cough,' said I.

'She might have consumption,' said the little girl.
'That's what my sister that died last year had. I'm
waiting for a tonic for my other sister. She have to
have tonics all the time. Is it nice where ye live?'

So I told her about the Glen, and she told me about
the river out to Carrigrohane. It seemed to be a
nicer place altogether than ours, the way she described it. She was a nice, talkative little girl and I
never noticed the time till the shutter went up and a
bottle was banged down on the counter.

'Dooley!' shouted the seedy man and the window
shut again.

'That's for me,' said the little girl. 'Yours won't be ready for a long time yet. I'll wait for you.'

'I have a lop,' I said, showing her my penny.

'Boy, we'll be able to get a bag of sweets for that.' I liked that little girl a lot. She restored my confidence. I knew now that I was exaggerating things and that the mother would be all right without any self-sacrifice on my part. We sat on the steps by the infirmary and ate the sweets. At the end of the lane was the limestone spire. All along it young trees over-hung the high walls, and the sun, when it came out in hot golden blasts behind us, threw our linked shadows out on to the road.

'Give us a taste of your bottle, little boy,' she said.

'Can't you taste your own?' I replied suspiciously.

'Ah, mine is awful,' she said with a mournful shrug. 'Tonics is awful. Try it, if you like.'

I did, and hastily spat it out. Awful was the word for it. But after that, I couldn't do less than let her taste mine. She took a long swig out of it that alarmed me.

'That's grand!' she said enthusiastically. 'I love cough bottles. Try it yourself and see.'

I did, and saw that she was right about that too. It was very sweet and sticky, like treacle, only with more bite in it.

'Give us another,' she said, grabbing at it.

'I will not,' I said in alarm. ' 'Twill be all gone.'

'Ah, don't be an old miser,' she said scornfully, with a curious pout. 'You have gallons of it.'

And somehow I couldn't refuse her. My mother was far away, and I was swept from anchorage into an

unfamiliar world of spires and towers, trees, steps
and little girls with red hair and green eyes. I
worshipped that girl. We both took another swig
and then I really began to panic.

'It's nearly all gone,' I said, beginning to snivel.
'What am I going to do now?'

'Finish it and say the cork fell out,' she replied as
though it were the most natural thing in the world,
and God forgive me, I believed her. We finished it
between us, and then, gradually as I put down the
empty bottle I remembered my mother sick and the
Blessed Virgin slighted, and my heart sank. I had
sacrificed both to a little girl, and she didn't even care
for me. It was my cough bottle she was after all the
time. Too late I saw her guile and burst into tears.

'What ails you?' she asked in astonishment.

'My mother is sick and you're after drinking her
medicine, and now if she dies 'twill be my fault,' I
said.

'Ah, don't be an old cry-baby!' she said contempt-
uously. 'You need only say that the cork fell out—
'tis a thing that might happen to anyone.'

'And I promised the Blessed Virgin a candle and I
spent it all on sweets for you!' I screamed, and away
with me up the road like a madman, holding the empty
bottle. Now, I had only one refuge and hope—a
miracle. I went into the cathedral to the shrine of the
Blessed Virgin, and having told her about my fall,
I promised her a candle with the very next penny I
got if only she'd make my mother better by the time I
got back. I looked at her face carefully in the candle-
light and I thought she didn't look too cross. Then I

crawled miserably back over the hill. All the light had gone out of the day, and the echoing hillside had become a vast alien, cruel world. As well as that I felt terribly sick after the cough bottle. It even crossed my mind that I might die myself. In one way it would be a great ease to me.

When I got home the silence of the kitchen and the sight of the empty grate showed me at once that the Blessed Virgin had let me down. The mother was still in bed. I couldn't bear it, and I began to howl.

'What is it at all, child?' my mother cried anxiously from upstairs.

'I lost the medicine,' I bellowed from the foot of the stairs and then dashed blindly up and buried my face in the bedclothes.

'Oh, wisha, wisha, wisha, if that's all that's a trouble to you, you poor misfortunate child!' she cried in relief, running her hand through my hair. 'Is anything the matter?' she added anxiously. 'You're very hot.'

'I drank the medicine,' I bellowed and then buried my face again.

'And if you did itself, what harm?' she murmured soothingly. 'You poor child! Going all that way by yourself, without a proper dinner or anything, and to have your journey for nothing. Undress yourself now, and rest here for a while.'

She rose, put on her slippers, and her overcoat and unlaced my boots while I sat on the bed. Even before she was finished I was fast asleep. I didn't see her dress herself or hear her go out, but some time later I felt a hand on my forehead and saw Minnie Ryan peering down at me, laughing.

'Arrah, 'tis nothing, woman,' she said lightly. 'He'll sleep that off by morning. Aren't they the divil? The dear knows, Mrs. Sullivan, 'tis you should be in bed.'

I knew. I knew it was her judgment on me; I was one of those that were more savages than Christians; I was no good as a nurse, no good as anything. I accepted it all. But when my mother came up with her paper and read it beside my bed, I felt I could afford to let them all despise me, because there was one who didn't. My prayer was answered. The miracle had happened.

L. A. G. STRONG

THE GATES

L. A. G. Strong was born in 1896 at Plymouth, of Irish parents. Much of his boyhood leisure was divided between the Devon moors and the Irish countryside near Dublin, where he spent his holidays. He was educated at Brighton College and Wadham College, Oxford. He taught for twelve years at an Oxford preparatory school, until the success of his first novel, Dewer Rides, *encouraged him to give up teaching and devote all his time to writing. His best-known novels are* The Brothers *and* The Bay; *he has also achieved a high reputation as a writer of short stories and has written and broadcast much about poetry and the speaking of poetry. He is a visiting tutor at the Central School of Speech and Drama, a member of the Irish Academy of Letters, and a director of Messrs. Methuen and Co. Ltd., the publishers. He says that his recreations are music, walking in the country and talking dialect.*

●

CRASH!

Old Sam Henniker leaped up in his bed, knowing on the instant what had happened: the 7.1 had fouled the gates. He knew at once, because he had dreamed the disaster scores of times, starting bolt upright, to be reassured by darkness and quiet all around. But this was more terrible than the dream: over and above the splintering of wood and the grind of lacerated metal came a fearful bumping, a thud which shook the house, and, at the end of all, a forlorn tinkle of broken glass.

She'd fouled the gates. He must have overslept horribly. Then his alarum-clock had not gone off. Shaking from head to foot he tumbled out of bed and ran over to it. Peering at it in the half-light, he saw, with a cold, sick feeling, that it had not been set over-night. And all this in a few seconds: the steam of the train was still drifting sluggishly over the misty fields as Sam stood there in his nightshirt, the clock in his hand, staring upon tragedy.

He had forgotten to set the clock. That was worse, to Sam, than the disaster it had entailed. Punctual, accurate, regular in his habits as a machine, he had always switched off the alarum on getting up each morning, lest in the afternoon it should disturb the house with an unmeaning summons; and reset it before going to bed at night. He had done it for more years then he could reckon. And last night, suddenly, inexplicably, he had gone to bed without setting it—had overslept—and the 7.1 had fouled the gates.

But he was a railwayman still; and so he roused himself quickly, slipped on his coat, trousers, and peaked cap, and went down to survey the damage. In the grey wet morning light it was plain to see. Above the crossing the line curved, which prevented the driver of the train from getting a view of the gates till he was almost upon them. Of course, he should whistle, but there were few formalities on the little single line, and Sam's reputation for punctuality would in any case have been his own undoing: moreover, even if the driver had whistled, it would have been too late. The train had evidently taken the obstacle at full speed. One gate—the second—had been flung bodily aside, and seemed to have suffered little damage: but the other was dashed to pieces. The heavy post, torn from its socket in the ground and dragged for several yards by its twisted metal bar, had smashed a corner of the fence and fetched up against Sam's oilhouse; that accounted for the bumping noise. Bits of metal and wood were scattered all about the line; there was a great scar across the painted woodwork of the little ground frame hut, and its window was broken. Even then Sam wondered that in the midst of such huge destruction he should have heard this little sound so clearly.

Well, his job was plain before him. The metals were clear, but he proceeded to move any fragments that might possibly be in the way of the upcoming train, and then turned back to the house to dress.

At the door he was met by his little grandson, with white wondering face and round eyes. The boy looked up at him, and his lips moved in silent question.

'Train. Fouled gates,' said Sam gruffly, with a funny backward swing of his arm towards the disaster; and he brushed past the boy and stumped upstairs.

As he lathered his chin before the little cracked glass by the window, he heard the arrival of Mrs. Jarvis who 'did' for them. 'Oooh my!' she said. 'Wattever——'

He lost the rest, but could hear the boy's voice answer her, and their hushed voices as they gazed upon the destruction. Sam gritted his teeth. Then he heard her, as usual, moving about in the kitchen, getting the breakfast ready.

A few minutes later, he was sitting opposite his grandson at the table, outwardly as much the martinet as ever; but he found it hard to meet the boy's eyes. Never troubling, as a rule, to read another's thought, he could see criticism grow each moment in his grandson's mind. Grandfa, so punctual, so unfailing, so merciless to the slovenly or forgetful; grandfa, by whom the people set their clocks of a Saturday as he went down to the village for his evening glass— grandfa had overslept, and let the train smash up the gates. Grandfa had made a terrible mistake. Grandfa. The child's world rocked upon its foundation. Slowly, with the full tide of inevitable knowledge, he was learning that grandfa was only a man, an ordinary man, liable as any other man to make mistakes. And the old man saw it all, and suffered torments. He wanted to say: 'Swally up thy porridge, don't thee stare to me!' but somehow he could not. Still, age was age, and right was right; so presently, with a real effort of courage, he looked up and met the accusing eyes.

'Come along with 'ee,' he said gruffly. ' 'Tis getting late.'

The boy's eyes dropped at once, and he finished up the remains of his porridge. After that they did not speak at all; and the boy, as soon as they left the table, got his satchel and started off for school guiltily. He saw already that the disgrace would affect him as well, that there would be questions to answer, and jeers to bear; and suddenly he realized that he loved his grandfather, and longed to defend him. He had always spoken, at school, as if the work of the crossing was shared between them. 'Us lets train through,' he would say, and describe the process in detail to an interested circle. Well, this morning, what would he say? 'Us overslept, and train fouled gates.'

'Grandfa overslept . . .

'Grandfa forgot to set the clock, so us over-slept . . .

'Us forgot to set the clock . . .'

No; there was no need to go that far; he was always in bed long before the clock was set. 'Grand-fa . . .' 'Us . . .' He shuffled along the lane, in the gutter, struggling. . . .

As soon as Mrs. Jarvis, frightened and constrained, had hurried the breakfast-things from the table and shut the scullery door behind her, the old man sat with his pipe unlighted, and tried to cope with the disaster which had befallen him. It was as if a devil had flung into the regularity of his life this unforeseen and unbelievable horror. He was a good, steady man; said his prayers daily to the Lord and attended meeting regularly; more than that, there was a class of boys who assembled respectfully, every Sunday afternoon, to hear Mr. Henniker expound the Word of God. Bruised and bewildered, he searched his conscience, and could find no sin, no backsliding, to warrant this cruel visitation. ' 'Tis a dream,' he thought, and half rose from his chair; but even through the window he could see enough, and he sat down again.

The 8.40 up found Sam, as ever, in the little ground frame hut, looking grimly out at the broken window. He heard it whistle, excessively and ostentatiously, below the straight, and set his jaw. There would be a deal of this sort of thing to face. They'd have had a fine tale, down at the station; they'd none of them be sorry to get one in on old Sam Henniker. Old Sam, who had refused to come out on strike; who had argued so uncompromisingly, in the bar of the Blue Boar, against shorter hours, the modern labouring man, the unpunctuality and thriftlessness of the young; oh, they'd have it in for old Sam all right. But Joe the driver, as he passed, made him a face of comic dismay, in which there was no unkindness. 'Well, you 'ave been and gone and done it, and no mistake,' the face said, not without sympathy; and, to his amazement, Sam instinctively made a grimace in return. Then he was angry with himself for wanting sympathy.

Traffic on the road was limited to bakers' carts and a farmer or two on a nag; but today, these, stopping at the crossing, gaping at the damage, and commenting thereon, made up by concentration for their lack of numbers. Never had the place seemed so populous. Sam eyed them grimly; they speculated among themselves upon the causes of the disaster, looking sideways at him, but none ventured to ask the old man a direct question.

That afternoon, Sam sat down and penned his official report of the accident. It was brief and bare:

the work of a proud man, humble in so far as he was at
fault, but neither asking for, not expecting, pardon.
In his own eyes the offence was unforgivable. He
would show no mercy to a subordinate who had
committed it, and he found none for himself. His
one duty had been to keep the line clear for six trains
a day, and he had failed to do so. Thirty years of such
service, ever since the line was opened, counted in
his mind for nothing. It was the unpardonable offence,
and, by some mysterious fate which he could not
understand, he, of all men, had committed it.

It was not till two days afterwards that a gang
arrived to put up a new pair of gates. Sam, fearing
men who knew him, was relieved to see a regular
gang from a town quite thirty-five miles distant. He
found, with something of a shock, that they took the
accident much as a matter of course. They talked of
other things; and when he fought down his pride
sufficiently to ask if they had much work of the kind,
they reassured him with ready sympathy. Bless him,
yes. Why, one gate on the Tilton line had been
broken twice inside three months.

'You won't get the sack, master, not as 'tis the
first time,' added one, misunderstanding him.

Sam stiffened all over, went abruptly into the
house, and sat on a chair in the kitchen. He would
have liked to be angry: he ought to have been angry,
he told himself fiercely, and put the young chap in
his place; yet in some curious way his heart could
not help recognizing the rough kindness, and being
grateful for it.

'Takes it 'ard, 'e do,' said one of the men to

another; and when, presently, they laughed over
another matter, Sam savagely supposed that they
were laughing at him, and marched down to the
farthest corner of his neat vegetable garden to be out
of sight and hearing.

The next day was Saturday, Sam's evening for
visiting the inn. He spent the day fighting his fears.
All would laugh and sneer at him. For long years he
had checked and censured them, so stern with himself, so unfailing in his own life that they could not
grudge his right to find fault. Now he had failed. But
to stay away would be cowardice. He became angry,
unfair. Why need he mind them, the trash? What
did it matter what they said? And he stumped
fiercely down the long hill to the village.

He was right—there was a change. Women,
gossiping at their doors in the soft failing light,
hushed their voices and stared at him—with pity,
could he have seen it. Children playing in the gutters
paused to look, with open mouths. The unhappy
man, his eyes fixed on his road, felt as if heads and
mocking voices were closing in behind him, dark and
chuckling, as the waters close behind a boat at night-
fall. He reached the inn; for just a second he hesitated
on the sandy threshold, then entered boldly.

He scarcely noticed who was in the bar. There was
a group in one corner. He ordered his glass, and sat
lonely on the big settle farthest from the fire, which
had just been lit, and was burning brightly but
indecisively. There had been a murmur of greeting
as he came in, and he had heard himself answer.
Misery crushed and scalded him. He had felt little

in his life—not since Ann had died; never anything shameworthy, like this; he was not accustomed to such suffering, and he bore it hard. They were talking among themselves. A curse rose suddenly and bitterly in old Sam's heart. Ordinarily it would have shocked him, for he never swore. Yet it came naturally now. Well, let them talk, the—! He suddenly realized that he had drunk all his beer, without tasting it, and that his mouth was still dry and thirsty. His eyes smarted, and a pain ran down his side and down his legs. Then there was a movement in the group, and a man approached and stood over him—Jim Watkins. Sam turned up to him a face of animal defiance.

'Sam,' said the man, 'come and have a drink with us, and cheer thee up.'

Sam swallowed with stiff jaws, and looked at him without speaking. A second man rose from the group, and joined Watkins.

'You've had a misfortin', Sam,' he said, 'and us be sorry for't. You'm a proud man, a steady-going man, and nobody likes to 'ave their mistakes spoke much of, you least of all. Still, 'tis a misfortin', and us be sorry; and us would take it very kind if you would come and have a drink with us, in token of goodwill.'

Tears rose to the red rims of Sam's eyes. It was dead against his principles to take a second glass, but he must now. His heart warmed to the men.

'Thank 'ee,' he answered huskily; 'you're very kind, and I'll be glad.'

An hour later he was on his way home, walking furiously fast, as ever, his heart warm with gratitude and an unaccustomed heat of liquor. For the first

time since the crash, he felt almost happy. It wasn't
so bad after all. He had misjudged the good folk
sinfully: he must pray to be forgiven that. Kind folk
they were. Tears came to his eyes, happy tears, for
the drink had made him emotional, and his quick
steps were a little unsteady. Every one made a
mistake sometimes. It wasn't so bad. He stamped his
feet hard on the rough road, and took the steep finish
of the hill at a pace which few young men in the
district could have equalled. He came out upon the
dark moor above the crossing; a bullock was lying
in the road, and he bore down upon it. 'Hoy!' he
barked, and the animal rose lumberingly and let him
pass. He even whistled a few long-forgotten notes, as
the shape of the house loomed up, and the white paint
of the new gates showed faint and ghostly in the
darkness.

The next morning he felt ill, and would have liked
to stay away from meeting; yet that, again, would
seem cowardice. He put down his cup, seized with a
sudden fear that some one might be inspired to pray
in his behalf. A sweat stood out on him, and he
gulped his tea blindly. Then reason came back. They
might do it if he were away, but far less likely if he
were there. They wouldn't have the brass, he thought,
with a gleam of his old spirit. So he went off with his
grandson trotting at his side, and sat and knelt with
throbbing head, his fears ebbing from him as the
service wore on to its end.

He went to bed early that night, to be in readiness
for the morrow. The alarum was left permanently
set now: its tinkle, feeble in the daylight, sounded

every afternoon, half comforting, half worrying him. The passing of the trains was getting on his nerves. He dared scarcely let himself go off to sleep now. Suppose the alarum went wrong, did not work? It had failed once, many years before, but without evil consequence. He had cured it by putting it in the big vat of paraffin oil from which the lamps were filled. There it had lain for three weeks, till the supply ran out, and had been rescued in perfect order, but with a face the colour of brown paper; and it had behaved magnificently ever since. (Sam, incidentally, had caused much annoyance by his invariable recommendation of this treatment for all the deranged clocks in the neighbourhood.) Well, it had answered his own; why not? The clock had kept time ever since. But suppose it should fail again? It was old: clocks wore out. He sat up in his bed, and listened to its strong tick-tock on the chest of drawers. That was all right. He lay down again, slept perhaps a little, and woke with a start. Was it fancy, or did the ticking sound weaker? Ah—it seemed to falter then. And so on, and so on, up and down, like a head bobbing on the sea of consciousness, now under, now up again.

In the small hours he leaped and listened, trembling. No; all was still. He had dreamed his old dream again.

After that he could not sleep, nor even stop trembling. He lay flat on his back, gripped the bed-clothes, and jammed his feet against the end of the bed in his efforts at control, but his shaking only stopped when his muscles ached from the tension, and he lay sorely tired, his eyes burning in their sockets, wishing for day.

When the alarum did go off it woke him with a
shock: he must have just dropped off.   He lay a
minute, and almost went to sleep again.   Frightened,
he dressed unsteadily, yawning and blinking, and
stood in the ground frame hut, when the train went
through, a sick old man.

The new gates were finished.   Neighbours, coming
to look at them, were kind.   Why, they declared, it
was a good thing he had let the train go through the
old ones.   Company would have had to replace them
soon, anyway.   He had only speeded 'em up a bit.   And
the new Sam listened almost wistfully, with a smile,
to the nonsense which he would so fiercely have
rebuked ten days ago.

'Have improved old Sam no end, that there
accident have,' was the local verdict.   'Much more
'uman it have made en.'

'Aha.   Nothin' like misfortuin to bring a man in
line with his fella bein's.'

'Or a 'oman, too.'

'O' course, Joe.   I meaned a 'uman, not only a
male man.'

'Aw.'

But Sam was losing in vitality what he gained in
gentleness of heart.   The nights, which had been
brief intervals of unbroken sleep, were now long
shivering ages, broken by hideous dreams.   Gigantic
engines shrieked along the line: he would run to
open the gates, but always fail.   Sometimes the
lighted train, with a rending as of the crack of doom,
would rush grinning by: at other times it would bear
down upon him as he struggled with the gates—be

on top of him—the crash would be all about him—
and he would wake with shut quivering eyelids,
convinced that he was dead, and become wearily
conscious of his body still whole and aching on the
bed. Soon he came to pray that he might not awaken,
but that the dream-train might finish all.

His thin face grew thinner, and yellow; his eyes
were sunken in his head, their red rims redder than
ever; his hand shook as he hung up the lamp upon each
gate, and he became gentle and weary, like a sick dog.
For the first time in many, many years, he missed
Ann. She would have looked after him. On the few
occasions when he was ill in her lifetime, he had
been a crotchety invalid, and she gentle, patient, and
firm, laughing and soothing him out of his tantrums.
'Twould be easier for her now. And then he remembered that, if she were alive, she would be old like
himself, and not the girl of those days . . .

Memories, sights and sounds and touches forgotten, were coming back to him. A white comb and
thick, dark hair. A warmth at night, and murmured
words. He smiled through his pain in the darkness, and
felt something of the sunshine of long buried days.
Then pain conquered: he was alone.

'Ann,' he whispered. Then, louder: 'Ann.'

He coughed, and fell asleep. When the alarum woke
him, after several hours, he felt very tired, but happier,
as if something more than sleep had made the hours
good. That was Friday morning. He coughed a lot
in the afternoon, and the next night his legs would
not carry him to the village for his visit to the inn.

On Sunday he had a pain in his chest and felt light-headed; and the next morning, when he awoke in fearful pain, it was broad day, and there were people in the room. A sudden dread stabbed him; he tried to struggle up, but could not speak.

'It's all right,' the doctor told him quickly, 'the gates were opened all right. No harm done.'

Sam sank back. Then a slow question formed between his puzzled eyes. His lips shaped it painfully.

'Who?'

'The boy—your grandson. He couldn't waken you, so he did it himself, and sent word down for me. A rare good boy, that.'

A blank: afternoon light. The evening star shining very clearly in at the open window: open much wider than usual. The doctor had had the window-sash taken right out. A large fire roared in the grate. Shadows leaped on the wall . . . sometimes they were friendly, sometimes terrible, like engines rushing down on him . . . A poultice—on his back. Ah-h.

He was young again. He and Ann wandered by the seashore, and picked up shells. She had bare feet. They came into a little corner of the rocks, and he kissed her. She laughed happily, and they walked slowly along, his arm around her waist. They talked a lot. He tried to remember what they said, to tell the nurse. It was a wonderful plan they had made, but he could not remember any of it.

On Wednesday morning a letter came from the company. They had deliberated upon his case, and, serious though his breach of duty had been, in consideration of his otherwise unblemished record they had decided to continue him in his post without fine or prejudice to his pension.

Neighbours made several attempts to read Sam this document, but they could not be sure whether he understood it. He seemed happy, and whispered to himself from time to time; but it was not clear if he knew where he was, or heard what was said to him.

'He must have took it in; he seems so happy, like,' whispered his daughter-in-law.

' 'Twould ha' broke his heart if company had gived en the sack, or retired en.'

'Doctor don't think he've heard a word not since early dawn.'

So the question remained unsolved, and Sam died at about five o'clock that afternoon. Neighbours talked far into the night, searching out the justice and the meaning of it all: whether, if such an accident had happened earlier in his life, it would have softened him, without proving mortal. Just as he had become human and fit for society, he had been taken from it. They wondered what difference it would have made had his wife lived, and asked each other many such questions. They felt little personal grief, only a pleasant warmth of sorrow; they wished they could have shown some especial kindness to the old man, and they felt aware of life's strangeness and mystery.

The low hum of their voices sounded outside the house. The orange light in the parlour window showed brighter than usual, and occasionally a head could be seen moving across the blind. A man on a horse passed down the road, and wondered idly at the sound of voices. It was bright moonlight; the metals gleamed, and the new gates showed very white and clear.

QUESTIONS

QUESTIONS

GENERAL

1. Pick out three stories which have effective openings and show what makes them effective.
2. In which stories in this book is a neatly-contrived ending an important feature of the plot?
3. In which stories are incidents and characters presented from *outside*? Choose one of these and show what we learn of the writer's attitude to his characters.
4. Which of these stories are primarily: (*a*) heroic, (*b*) comic, or (*c*) realistic? What makes them so?
5. What experience do we gain from this book of: (*a*) war, (*b*) childhood, (*c*) other people's work and play?
6. In which of the stories are you conscious of the prose style? What qualities in style give you pleasure or irritate you?
7. In which stories is a local atmosphere important? How is it suggested?
8. Are there any stories here where the events matter less than other elements, such as ideas or atmosphere?
9. Which story do you like most and which do you like least? Give reasons.
10. Show from this collection the wide range of matter and form covered by the term 'short story'.

SERGEANT CARMICHAEL

1. What forms of heroism are shown in this story?
2. What is the purpose and the effect of the peace-time memories recalled by Johnnie and Carmichael?
3. Is there a plot in this story?

THE HALF-MILE

1. By what details does the writer convey the sensation of nervous tension before the race?
2. Show how the whole atmosphere changes for Andrew after his victory.
3. How does the style reflect the changing course of events?
4. How can you tell that the author has been a runner himself?

CAESAR'S WIFE'S EAR

1. Show how the intensity of emotions among human beings—love, jealousy, loyalty — is paralleled among the lions.
2. How far do qualities of style—sentence-structure, vocabulary and striking metaphor—help to create the atmosphere of heat and tension?
3. How does the author contrive to make us care deeply what happens to Seppel?
4. Explain the appropriateness of the title.

THE PRODIGAL CALF

1. What is the meaning of the title?
2. What features of the ordinary life of soldiers on active service help to form a setting for this story?

JUMPING FOR JOY

1. What points of resemblance are there between this story and 'The Half-Mile'?
2. Is this really a short story? Has it a plot?
3. What contribution to the effect of the story is made by (a) variation of sentence-construction and rhythm, (b) unexpected verbs, and (c) metaphor and simile?
4. How far is the title: (a) ironical, (b) ambiguous?

THE EXAMINATION FOR LIEUTENANT

1. What do we learn of conditions of service in the Navy 150 years ago?
2. 'He was being borne along on a wave of the highest exaltation; the roar of the fire was intoxicating, and he knew not a moment's fear.' Describe the actions of Hornblower that justify Forester in writing this about him.

SATURDAY AFTERNOON

1. Why is it that we begin by disliking the Spenk family and end by sympathizing rather than blaming?
2. The story is full of detail that appears trivial but is really important to the author's purpose. Give examples.
3. Describe the structure of this story. Is it one or three?
4. Is your interest here mainly in incident—i.e. in what happens next? If not, what is the main source of interest?

A MAN AND A FOX

1. What impression do you form of the writer? To what extent does he appear to laugh at himself?
2. How does he gain, as the story goes on, in sensitiveness and in understanding of Nature?
3. Which moments are most vividly imagined and narrated?

RETURN OF THE MOON MAN

1. This is science fiction told by a simple child from a backward area. Is the author making fun of science fiction or of the rural Welsh, or both?
2. The Moon-Ship lands in Ten Acre Field; one of the Moon Men, having bitten his tongue, wants to catch the next train back to Golders Green; Grandfather, back from the Moon, wants to know if the fence has been mended. Find more examples of the world of space-travel side by side with the humdrum.
3. How does the Welsh idiom contribute to the effect of the story?

WANTED—A MIRACLE

1. Why is a Welsh setting important and how is it suggested?
2. Would the story be strengthened or weakened if Dilys did not achieve success in another sphere?
3. Consider the style, particularly in the use of simile and metaphor.

THE MAN OF THE HOUSE

1. Which parts of the story are: (*a*) comic, (*b*) moving? What is particularly amusing about the conclusion?
2. In which moments of the story does the author most intensely capture the *feel* of being a child?
3. What is Irish about the story?
4. In what sense is the title appropriate?

THE GATES

1. How have Sam Henniker's past virtues contributed to his collapse?
2. In what way is the grandson important in the story?
3. What feelings are stirred in the reader by the last paragraph?